BEAUTY N' BETRAYAL

SINCERE

TRJ
PUBLISHING

TRJ Publishing
P.O. Box 3342
Culver City, CA 90230-9998
www.BeautyNbetrayal.com

ISBN: 0-9889585-9-7 (pbk)
ISBN: 978-0-9889585-9-3 (ebook)
Library of Congress Control Number: 2013904168

Ordering Information:
Quantity sales. Special discounts are available on quantity purchases by corporations, associations, and others. For details, contact the publisher at the address above.

Editor: Shontrell Wade
Cover design: Sincere and Patrice Johnson
Cover photograph: Patrice Johnson
Author photograph: www.ronibrown.com

The Author is available for speaking engagements. For more information or to book an event contact TRJ Publishing at info@beautyNbetrayal.com
Manufactured in the United States of America

10 9 8 7 6 5 4 3 2 1

This book is dedicated to my beautiful daughters, Tatierra and Patrice, my parents, Mary and Troy, and to the memory of my aunts Enetta and Mae and uncle Joe.

I also dedicate this book to all the dreamers and procrastinator out there like I was. Trust me, the moment you decide to "JUST DO IT and LET GO AND LET GOD" is the second you'll start to succeed, live and truly be happy!

Ackonwledgements

All praise to my Lord and Savior, Jesus Christ. I am nothing without you; in all things I give glory to you God.

My testimony: In November 1991, eight days before my birthday, my best friend, P.J., was killed. Two weeks later, his killer robbed me at gunpoint. I lost my faith in God. Furious, I walked around saying there's no God, cursing him and questioning his existence. "If he exists, why are innocent people and children getting killed, raped, abused, and born with defects?"

In March of 1995, I was six month pregnant and had a 1 ½-year-old daughter. I lost my apartment and had to move back in with my mother. On my third night living there, I said the most ignorant prayer in the world. "God if you are real, which I don't think you are, you will help me get a place for me and my children to live. And I don't know how you're going to do that because I don't have any money or job. Amen." That night, I had a dream about P.J. and I getting off the green line train on 35th. I was clueless as to why I dreamt that. Within in a week of my prayer and dream, I moved into a subsidized two-bedroom apartment on 36th and Michigan. Needless to say, my faith in God was immediately restored and I learned the power of prayer. God had to do something miraculous in my life to show me that he's real and worthy of my prayers. He saved this lost soul and made me a believer!

I did it! Hooray for the procrastinator. LOL. This book would not have been possible without the support and encouragement of my cousin, Keisha, who read my movie script and encouraged me to turn it into a book, daughter Tatierra and cousin Waddell (Boobie) putting the pressure on me to complete it, and my pastor Yvonne giving me God's word. Thanks and I love you all!

Thanks to my beautiful, intelligent, and talented daughters, Tatierra and Patrice—my strength and wisdom—for keeping me eager, ambitious, and determined. Without you girls, I'm incomplete. A person never truly knows their strength until they become a parent. Thanks to my parents, Mary and Troy. I know I drove you both crazy at one point or another, thanks for blessing me with your creativity, business minds, flare for fashion, giving spirits, tenacity, strength, and good looks. ;) I love you both unconditionally. My siblings (Hannah and Danas), my nephews (Shaquille and Adonis) my nieces (Sadai and Sydney-Hannah), and little cousins (too many to name), I do everything with you guys in mind. I hope I serve as an inspiration to you that anything is possible with commitment, faith in yourself, and God. I love you all! Thanks and love to my Woods and Lee families, it's because of you all that I am the person who stands today. A special thanks to my Auntie Virginia for being the backbone of the Lee family, being there for me and teaching me at a early age the strength, history, and importance of black people and showing me by example how to be an involved auntie; to Uncle Gerry for being my friend, security, and banker. LOL. Uncle Tommy for installing in me the importance of an education at an early age, Auntie Jean for teaching me early that there's consequences behind my actions (old fashion butt whooping's), Auntie Annie for telling me that my spirit makes me beautiful. Cousin Roscoe for having my back, giving me advice and a car, and Cousin Shavon for helping me with editing and proofreading this book, Cousin Sebrina, whose sassiness and beauty I've always admired, for showing me by example that it is possible to change your life at any age. Cousin, your strength became mine. When people tell me I can't, I think of you and say, "Oh, but yes, I can!" I love you all dearly. Thanks to my friends Olympia, Toleda, Francine, Zakiya, Lakita, Tocarra, Sonja, Cateye, Patrick, Marc, Victor Lord, Shawn, Duke, and J.J. I love you all. Dila, my friend whom I shared my deepest desire with, I love you and will continue to pray for you my brother. Author N'tyse, I could not have gotten this far without your support and guidance. Words cannot describe my gratitude to you. Shontrell Wade, thank you for having the patience of Job and going above and beyond your editing duties.

Thanks to my spiritual advisor Pastor Yvonne and my prayer friend Katrina, Mr. and Mrs. Hall, pillars in the Chatham community and my role models, Ms. Stewart for taking a chance on me. Mrs. Dianne Robinson for feeding, sheltering, and treating me like I was her child. My L.A. peeps, The Morrises, Davises, Branda and Nelson's for giving me the feel of a family presence.

To my Sincere Apparel Catwalk Divas, Cain, Donna, Latrina, Angel, Pie-Pie, Pamela, Dazja, A.J. , Anna and Tracey. Thanks for helping a sista out and bringing life to my apparel! Thanks to all my Social Site friends and Sincere Apparel clients for your support over the years.

To my auntie Enetta, Aunt Mae, Uncle Joe, Granddaddy Thomas, and best friends, Jacqueaz and P.J., It saddens me that you guys aren't here to celebrate another accomplishment with me, but I know you all are my angels and cheering me on from above. R.I.P, my loves.

Chapter 1

"So, tomorrow's your big day, huh?"

Dino's six-foot-two frame lay sprawled across the king-sized bed.

Keisha smiled and continued flipping through the magazine she'd been reading. "Yes, baby, it is. And I can't wait."

"Yeah, but you haven't thanked me yet."

Confused, she turned to look at her boyfriend. "Thank you for what, baby?"

"Thank me for who you are."

"What do you mean?" She frowned.

"Before me, you weren't shit. Now look at you. You wear designer clothes, live in a fly-ass crib, and you ridin' in a slick whip. Hell, if I put you on the market, I'd make a killin' off yo ass. I made you a hot commodity," he gloated, sitting up and double-slapping his chest. Picking up a blunt from the nightstand, he lit it and took a pull. He looked at her, blowing thick white smoke from his mouth.

"You're the envy of every bitch," he continued

This bastard acts like I'm not even human, she thought.

"Not to mention you have me." He puffed out his chest. "So thank your king."

Not wanting a confrontation, instead of telling him how she really felt, Keisha put the magazine down and got up from the chaise she'd been sitting on. Walking over to the bed, she straddled Dino and looked straight into his eyes.

"Thank you, King. Thank you for everything that you've done for my mother and me. I love you." She kissed him on the lips.

"That's sweet, baby, but it ain't enough."

Sighing inwardly, she started kissing his chest, slowly making her way down.

"No, that ain't what I want either," he said, pushing her away.

Keisha didn't know what to do. A head session usually placated him. "What do you want, my king? Your wish is my command," she whispered, nibbling on his earlobe.

"I want you to crawl for me."

"Crawl?" she said, sitting up and laughing in disbelief.

"Do it look like I'm jokin'? Get on your knees and crawl!"

"Dino, I'm not crawling. I'll do whatever else you want, but I'm not getting down on the floor like an animal."

That's exactly what you're going to do, bitch, he thought, taking another pull of his blunt.

"When I met you, you and your mother were about to get evicted," he said. "You ain't have shit. You barely had a pot to piss in or a window to throw it out of. Hell, you was stuffing tissue in your panties." He frowned in disgust. "I introduced you to pads and shit. I buy your clothes, your hygiene products, and keep your hair and nails on point. Before me, you just existed. I gave you life. I'm your God and I said crawl, bitch, so get on your fuckin' knees!"

Keisha stood up, disbelief in her eyes. "Dino, I was *fifteen*. What was I supposed to do? I wasn't old enough to work." She turned to walk away.

Dino quickly put out his blunt, jumped up, grabbed her by the arm, and threw her to the floor. She fell, hitting the side of her face on the edge of the nightstand. He grabbed the TV remote, and turned the volume up high.

Knowing what was coming next, Keisha curled into a fetal position, blocking her face and tightening her body as best she could.

Bending over her, Dino punched and kicked her while screaming, "Crawl, bitch, crawl." He grabbed her hair, wrapped it around his hand, and pulled her up off the floor.

Keisha tried her best to fight back, but she was no competition for Dino who was built like an NFL quarterback and weighed a solid 250 pounds. He gripped the back of her neck with his free hand, squeezing until she fell to her knees. Then he pushed her face into the cherry wood floor and roughly placed his knee in her back. Pain rocked her body like an avalanche.

He flipped her over onto her back and pinned her down, looking into her chestnut brown eyes. He felt an adrenaline rush as he watched the tears stream down the side of her pretty face. He felt no compassion.

Keisha's chest rose and fell rapidly. Twisting and

turning, she tried to break loose. Her attempts failed. The more she tried to break free, the tighter he gripped and twisted her wrists. Her 140-pound frame was no match for Dino. She was terrified, wondering what he was going to do to her. She'd never seen this look in his eyes before—they were empty and soulless. She prayed for mercy.

Dino was determined to get her to submit to what he wanted. He grew more furious with her resistance. Bending down to her ear, he growled, "Bitch, I will kill you. Do you hear me? Now, are you ready to crawl?"

Taking a deep breath, Keisha shook her head.

Dino's eyes widened. *This bitch is going to make me kill her. I'm going to show her ass.* Using his left arm to hold her down, he unbuckled his belt and pulled it free of its loops. Wrapping the piece of leather around her neck, he pulled her up off the floor. Frantic, she tried to break free, pulling at the belt and gasping for air, but he tightened it against her struggles.

Finally, he let her loose and she fell back to the floor. Pinning her down on her stomach this time, he began striking her with the belt. Keisha screamed in agony.

"Please stop," she pleaded.

He ignored her. Relentless, he continued to hit her

"Please, please don't hit me no more, I'll crawl for you," she mumbled.

Dino paused in mid swing, the belt raised. "What did you say? I didn't hear you. Speak the fuck up."

Keisha trembled with fear, her voice wavering. "I'll crawl for you. I'll do whatever you want me to. Just please don't hit me no more."

Dino turned her over and kissed her on the forehead.

"All of this could've been avoided if you would've just done what I told you from the beginning," he said, wiping the tears from her face.

Keisha stared up at him, her eyes still filled with tears. She didn't know the monster standing before her. They had fought before, but he'd never gone to this extreme.

"Now, crawl for your king." Dino said, stepping back.

She struggled to her knees, slipping on the fabric of her ripped silk nightgown. Her body ached with every movement. She held her head down, not looking at him. She felt ashamed, violated, helpless, and degraded. Silent tears fell as she started to crawl toward him.

"That's right, crawl for me."

He walked over to the video camera he kept set up in their bedroom and pressed the record button. Moving into its view, he ordered Keisha to crawl to him and kiss his feet.

Still crying, she crawled slowly across the floor. Defeated, she lowered her head and put her lips to one of his feet, then the other.

Dino watched her with a sly smile. Pulling out his dick, he told her to sit up. "I want you to lick it clean. Like a puppy licking his paw."

Bringing her head to his groin, she smelled the scent of another woman's pussy and gagged. She moved her head away. He grabbed her hair and forcefully placed her back in the position. Shaken and afraid for her life, she did what he commanded.

Now fully aroused, he pulled Keisha to her feet, ripped the remainder of her torn nightgown from her body, and threw her face down on the mattress. Yanking her legs open, he thrust savagely into her. She begged him to stop and struggled to get away, but it was no use. The more she cried and screamed, the more it excited him.

Sated after busting several nuts, he picked her up like a dirty rag and carried her into the master bathroom. Blood dripped down her legs and onto the floor, leaving a trail of crimson droplets. He dumped her into the tub and turned on the hot water, burning her feet. Reacting quickly, she reached up and moved the handle to the warm setting.

"Soak your ass for a minute, it'll feel better in the morning'. Then come wipe this blood off my fucking floor.

Holding his crotch, he turned and went back into the bedroom

An hour later, long after the water had turned cold, Keisha finally gathered enough strength to clean herself. Brushing her hair from her face with one hand, she felt pain near her right cheekbone. She stepped out of the tub and went to the mirror. A small cut under her eye was beginning to swell.

Grabbing a towel from the counter, she ran cold water on it and held it to the wound. Looking into the mirror, she didn't recognize the person with the battered face and swollen lip staring back at her.

If only she could go back to the life she'd had before the death of her father ten years ago.

Growing up, she never wanted for anything. Her father, Chico, had been one of the biggest drug lords in Chicago, running a heroin operation on the Southside. With connections in the Dirty South and on the East and West Coasts, he was the man in charge.

He was a savvy businessman who not only moved major weight, but had also run legitimate businesses.

He'd owned a lounge, cab service, car wash, a laundromat, and investment properties—both residential and commercial. His motto was "To succeed in life, you have to supply what the people need as well as what they desire."

Chico had converted one of his four-unit buildings into a beautiful six-bedroom, three-and-a-half bathroom house for his wife and daughter. It had two guest rooms, a game room, an office, a playroom for Keisha, a parlor for Keisha's mom, and a swimming pool. Friends and family were frequent guests. Chico's brother, Ray, and his two sons had even lived with them for a while.

Her father was a family man who was not only respected by men, but was adored by women. None of the ladies who threw themselves at him had a chance in the world of winning over his heart. Isabella, his gorgeous wife and Keisha's mom, was the head bitch in charge and the only woman he ever loved.

She had met Chico on a plane to New York City where she was going to sign a modeling contract with Ford Modeling Agency. They fell in love at first sight and Chico promised her the world if she'd be his wife. They married the next week and, true to his word, he provided her a life of glitz and glam. They'd been happy and living a luxurious lifestyle until he'd been killed.

Isabella was convinced that Ray, Chico's own brother, had killed her husband or had someone do it. She told Keisha how she'd had a weird feeling and had cried all day for no apparent reason, so she prayed about it and asked Chico to stay home with her. He obliged until he received a phone call from Ray, who was no longer allowed in their house after making a pass at her. Apparently, he had asked Chico to meet with him about something important. Isabella had always told Chico that Ray was jealous of him and couldn't be trusted. Chico refused to believe her, however, saying his little brother would never harm him. He left that night and never returned.

A week later, Isabella received a call saying her husband's remains had been found on a burned school bus in Harvey, Illinois. The autopsy report indicated he had been gagged and his hands and feet tied behind his back. His throat had been slit and he'd been shot point blank in the back of his head. Isabella hadn't been the same since.

Chico had tried numerous times to teach her how to run the honest part of the business in case something ever happened to him, but she'd refused to learn. She'd been unable to fathom life without him or the thought of his death. In her mind, he would always be there to provide for and protect her and Keisha.

Isabella and Keisha had lived okay for about a year, but because of poor money management and unscrupulous lawyers, they eventually lost everything. Without an education, work experience, or anything to fall back on, Keisha's mom was completely lost.

Isabella had learned one thing throughout her life, however—beauty and pussy were power within themselves. She knew that men love taking care of attractive women, but, even more so, they couldn't resist taking care of beautiful damsels in distress. With this in mind, she used her status as a beautiful, struggling single mother to find rich and powerful men to take care of her and Keisha. The relationships never lasted more than a few months at a time; the drug habit she'd developed after her husband death was too much for any of the men to handle. This caused her and Keisha to be homeless often, living from friend to friend's house.

"I miss you so much, Daddy," Keisha said aloud. A single tear rolled down her face. "Things would be so much better if you were here."

"What the hell are you doing in there?" yelled Dino. "Bring yo' ass out here and get in the bed. You know I can't sleep without you next to me."

Keisha snapped back to reality when she heard his voice. "Here I come," she said, her voice wavering.

Back in the bedroom, she scrubbed her blood off the floor before reluctantly climbing into bed.

Dino turned toward her and pulled her to him, kissing the back of her neck. "I love you, baby. Get some rest, tomorrow is your big day."

His touch made her flesh crawl. She knew it was time for her to leave. She needed to make an exit plan. She remembered an episode of Oprah about abused women. They said you have to have an escape plan or they'll find you. She'd thought about killing him and using the tape as evidence of her abuse, but she knew that would lead to severe consequences from both the law and the streets. Dino had made his mark in the streets of Chicago and had soldiers who would do anything for him.

While he snored loudly, Keisha brainstormed. Ideas fell into place and she knew exactly what she would do.

It seemed as if Keshia had just dozed off when she awoke to the sound of Isabella knocking on the bedroom door. "Wake up, Keisha. Today is your special day. Get up, sleepyhead. Do you hear me?"

"Yes, I hear you, Mom. Here I come."

Keisha nudged Dino. "Dino, get up and unlock the door. I need to get dressed and my clothes are downstairs. Come on, Dino, get up."

Dino groaned and rolled over. "Okay, okay, baby," he mumbled.

Stretching, he sat up, grabbed his boxers, and went into the bathroom. Keisha stood by the bedroom door waiting for him to enter the security code so she could open the door. After being robbed, he had become paranoid and installed various cameras around the inside and outside of the house, high tech security alarms on every door, and a special lock on the bedroom door that only he knew the code to.

"Dino, come on. I don't want to be late."

"Here I come," Dino said, yawning and rubbing his eyes. "Oh, damn, baby," he said when he looked at her face. "I'm sorry. I don't know what got into me. I smoked some new weed last night. That shit had me trippin'. I'm sorry."

Not as sorry as your bipolar ass is going to be, Keisha thought. "It's fine" she said. "Nothing a little MAC won't cover."

"Please forgive me."

"I forgive you. Now, get ready so we can go." She refused to get into a conversation about the night before, not wanting anything to mess up the day she'd been waiting a long time for.

"A'ight, but first I got a surprise for you." Dino walked over to the nightstand, pulled out a rectangular silver box, and handed it to her.

Keisha took the box and kissed him on the cheek "Thank you. Now, can you please open the door?"

"Aren't you gonna open it?"

"Yes, but not now. I'll open it after I get dressed." She needed to get ready and didn't have time to fawn over another expensive trinket he'd given her in an attempt to assuage his guilt and smooth things over with her.

"I think you may want to open it now," he said with a smile.

Keisha sighed and opened the box. Inside was a folded piece of paper.

"What's this?" she asked.

"Go to the window," Dino instructed.

Suspicious, she moved just close enough to see the trees outside.

"Yeah, baby, it looks beautiful out there," she said, then turned to walk away.

He pulled her back, turned her around, and told her to walk closer and look down.

Her heart raced. She didn't know what he was up to. She looked around the room, searching for something to defend herself with, but saw nothing useful. Stepping closer to the window, she closed her eyes and silently prayed. *Lord, please do not let this insane bastard throw me out this window.*

Taking a breath, she opened her eyes and looked down. Her mouth dropped open. Grinning, she turned quickly around. "Is that mine?"

"Yeah, baby, it's yours."

She picked the paper up out of the box and unfolded it. It was the title to a E350 coupe, with her name, Keisha Malina Lee, listed as the owner.

She jumped on Dino and hugged him tight, kissing him all over his face. Thoughts of the torture he'd put her through the last night were pushed to the back of her mind, replaced by the pearl white Benz parked in the driveway with a pink ribbon on top.

"I have to go show my Mom, Dino. Unlock the door, please."

"A'ight." He smiled as he punched in the five-digit code.

Keisha ran down the stairs and burst into her mother's room, waving the car title. Isabella turned, her smile disappearing when she saw her daughter's face.

"Mom, Dino bought me a Benz! Let's go check it out."

"Yeah, I know, baby, not now. What happened to your face?"

Keisha sighed. "Mom, you already know."

"Keisha, what did you do?"

Keisha stared at her mother, incredulous. "What do you mean, what did *I* do?"

"Keisha, baby, come sit down."

Keisha sat on the stool at the vanity as instructed and her mother began applying makeup to disguise the bruising.

"Why do you make him so upset?" Isabella asked. "Don't you like the house we live in? Your clothes and jewelry? The furs? Your new car? Do you like all the nice things he provides?"

"Yes, Mom, I do. But—"

"Then act like it."

"Is it my fault that he doesn't feel like a man unless he's hitting, kicking, or choking the shit outta me?"

"Watch your mouth, young lady!"

"I'm sorry, Mom."

Isabella finished applying foundation and picked up a powder compact. "No, that's not what I'm saying. No man should ever put his hand on a lady, but, unfortunately, some do. Some women push a man to it by putting their hands on him and some by their choice of words. Listen, honey, until you can provide this lifestyle for yourself, you have to deal with his bullshit. Life is about sacrificing, Keisha. You're grown now and I can't sugarcoat shit for you anymore. Do you think your father and I never fought? Well, we did. But I knew when to be submissive and when to be aggressive."

"I'm so submissive that it should be my name— Submissive Keisha."

Isabella paused. "Very funny, young lady, keep joking. I'm trying to get you ready to deal with the real world. Your looks will get you in the door, but your knowledge and attitude will keep you there. Knowing how to handle yourself in every situation will protect you. This world will fuck you, then spit you out if you let it. Never be the person that gets fucked, you do the fucking. Remember that!" She closed the compact and lifted her daughter's chin to admire her camouflage work. "Keisha, I know my habit sometimes gets the best of me, but I love you and always want the best for you. And, right now, Dino is what's best for you."

"I'll do better, Mom. I'll try not to make him upset. I'd better go get dressed. I love you." She kissed her mom on the cheek and dashed from the room.

"Tell Dino his breakfast is ready," Isabella called after her.

Keisha rolled her eyes. "Okay."

A few minutes later, Dino walked into the kitchen. Isabella stared at him. With one hand on her hip, she watched as he sat down at the table.

"I don't like what you did to my daughter's face. She

is not your punching bag."

"I know. She just makes me so mad at times. I promise I'll never hit her again."

"Good," she said. She poured him a cup of coffee and kissed him on his forehead before going to fix his plate.

Moments later, Keisha walked into the kitchen. "How do I look?"

She took three long strides and turned, modeling her off-white, one shoulder, Roberto Cavalli dress. Swarovski crystals embellishments on the form-fitting dress glistened and the slit on one side of the floor-length garment revealed a long, shapely leg when she walked.

"You look beautiful," Dino said. He'd seen her dressed up before, but today she was exquisite. His dick rose to salute her and he repositioned himself so they wouldn't notice.

Isabella's eyes filled with tears. "Baby, today is the third happiest day of my life. The first was when I met your father and the second was giving birth to you."

"Mom, please don't make me cry, I don't want to mess up my makeup. I have to go. Please be on time. It starts promptly at eleven and seating is limited."

"Are you driving your new car?" Dino asked.

She smiled. "You know I am."

"It's been a while since you've been behind the wheel, do you remember how?"

"Funny," she said dryly.

Isabella hugged her. "I know your father is smiling down on you from heaven."

Keisha kissed Dino and darted out the door. She walked around her new ride, checking it out. Of course,

Dino had it decked out and sitting on 20-inch rims. Opening the door and sliding inside, she saw that it was fully loaded—keyless start, leather steering wheel and interior, dual power heated seats, Bluetooth capability, panoramic sunroof, DVD/MP3 player, power rear window sunshade, automatic adjustable seats, four zone climate controls, and a navigation system. When she started the ignition, the engine purred. She smiled, adjusted the mirrors, and drove off.

She couldn't believe that she was driving by herself. It was something Dino never let her do. *He must really feel guilty*, she thought. She pulled out her cell phone to call Tameka and Sherrie.

The three girls had been best friends since their pigtail days. Their mothers used to be best friends too. But, like with most friends, men, money, drugs, or jealously had invaded and destroyed the friendship. Keisha, Tameka, and Sherrie were determined not to let any of those things come between them.

Using the car's Bluetooth, Keisha called Tameka.

"Hey, Tameka. What's up, girl?" she said when her friend answered.

"Nothing much, just getting ready. What time do we have to be there?"

"It doesn't start 'til eleven, but I'm coming to pick you guys up now."

"What? You're driving by yourself?" Tameka asked, shocked.

"Yeah. And guess what I'm driving?" Keisha sang.

"What?"

Keisha took a quick glance around her new ride. "A brand new—" She stopped when her eyes fell on the empty passenger seat, realizing she'd left her bag at home. "Damn."

"What's wrong?"

"I'll call you back. I left my bag at the house. I have to turn around."

"A'ight. I'll call Sherrie and tell her to come over. We'll be here waiting. Oh, and sis, in case I forget to tell you later, I am so proud of you."

"Thank you. That means a lot to me. I'll see y'all in a few minutes."

After hanging up, she made a quick u-turn and headed back to the house.

Keisha was ecstatic. Feeling on top of the world, she couldn't remember the last time she was so happy. Turning on the radio, she heard one of her favorite songs, a throw back. She turned up the volume and rapped along with Lil' Kim about berettas and amarettas, butta leathers, and mad cheddaz.

Pulling onto her block, she turned the radio off. Once inside the house, she yelled, "I forgot my cap and gown!"

There was no response, but she heard what sounded like moaning. She peeked inside her mother's room and saw no one was there. Nearing the stairway, the moaning became louder.

"Oh, Dino, you know what to do to make Momma happy."

Keisha ran up the stairs and pushed open the bedroom door.

Her man was down on his knees, kissing the place from where she had been birthed. She opened her mouth, but nothing came out. She stood frozen, unable to believe what she was seeing.

Chapter 2

*K*eisha trembled with anger, stunned beyond belief. Her arms fell to her sides, her knees went weak, and she slumped to the floor, crying silently.

Dino and Isabella were so into each other they didn't see or hear her. Her mind raced. She gathered her strength and went to the hall closet to get one of Dino's pistols. *I'm gonna kill these bitches*, she thought wiping the tears from her eyes.

Ransacking the closet, she came across a duffle bag filled with money, drugs and a scale. Seeing it brought her exit plan to mind. She hadn't planned to execute it so soon, but now was the perfect time. She tiptoed down the stairs, walked quietly to the kitchen, and spread the drugs out on the table. Next, she put a pot of water on the stove and placed baking soda and the scale next to a plate. It wasn't a large amount of cocaine, but enough to get Dino sent away.

She knew that he had two strikes against him and a third one would put him away for a long time. She also planted some in her mother's room on the dresser, figuring a district attorney would see Isabella as an addict and, since it was her first offense, would probably send her to a rehab center. Although her mother had betrayed her, Keisha didn't want her to go to jail.

Keisha quickly grabbed all the pictures of her and her father off the dresser in her mother's room. They were the only things in that house that meant anything to her. She stuffed them in the bag with the money and drove to the nearest pay phone.

"Nine-one-one, can I help you?" the operator asked.

Keisha deepened her voice to sound like a man. "Yeah, I want to report a drug deal going down. Hurry before they leave. This dude is someone you guys been trying to catch for a long time." She gave the address to Dino's house.

"Sir, what is your name?" the operator asked before Keisha dropped the phone receiver, leaving it to hang by its cord.

She hopped into her car and drove to the small alley across from her house. She parked the car and hid in the neighbor's bushes. Moments later, she watched the police bust in the door of her house and bring her mother out, handcuffed and crying hysterically. Keisha would have felt sorry Isabella if not for the sheet wrapped around her naked body. Her sympathy turned to anger. *That's what her dope fiend ass gets.*

Next, the officers brought out a half-naked Dino in handcuffs. From across the street, it looked like he had a smile on his face. He didn't seem worried at all.

Oh God, Keisha thought. *What if he gets off?*

The thought of Dino somehow evading jail time and actually getting out of the mess she'd concocted made her suddenly nervous.

After the police left, Keisha snuck back into the house.

Carefully stepping over things the police officers had tossed aside, she came across a box of videotapes in the closet. She took the box, then went into the bedroom and got the camcorder and everything else she could think of that would humiliate her if anyone found them. Finally, she grabbed the title to her car and left.

After she'd driven some distance away from the house, Keisha pulled over on the side of the road to see what was on the tapes. She'd known he liked to tape them, but she hadn't known just how many times he'd taped them when she'd been unaware. *Was this bastard recording us every time?* She watched the tapes in disgust. Horrified, she saw that Dino had not only taped their sex encounters, but he'd also captured the numerous times he'd been with her mother.

Her cell phone rang.

"Who the hell is this calling me?" she asked, searching through her purse for the phone. Finally recovering it, she looked at the caller ID and saw it was Tameka.

"Where are you? We've been sitting outside waiting."

Keisha cried as she told Tameka everything that had just happened.

"Come get us right now, Keisha. You don't need to be alone."

"Here I come." Keisha hung up.

After transferring several stacks of money from the duffel bag to her purse, she put it, the camera, and the box of tapes in the trunk. Putting the car in drive, she headed to her friend's house.

"What happened?" Sherrie asked, firing questions at Tameka. "What's wrong with Keisha? Did that punk put his hands on her again?" Tell me what's wrong. What's going on?"

"Keisha just caught Dino and her mother having sex," Tameka explained.

"What?" Sherrie flopped down on the sofa with her mouth wide open. "Are you serious?"

"Yes." Tameka nodded. "Not only that, she found a stash of videotapes that Dino had. Apparently, they've been sexing since they all moved out there." She shook her head in disbelief.

"So they've been screwing for two years?" Sherrie asked, astonished at what she was hearing.

"I want to seriously hurt that trifling-ass bastard for putting her through this shit."

"Don't worry, every dog has his day. But how could her *mother* do that to her?" Sherrie huffed. "So that explains why she never told Keisha to leave his sorry ass."

"Keisha's mother is strung out. Everybody knows that a crack-head will do anything for a fix. Hell, they got straight men sucking dick for a high. Besides that, Keisha's mom still looks good for her to have a habit. Hell, she and Keisha look just alike. That trifling-ass Negro took advantage of her."

Just then, a car horn sounded from in front of the house. The two quickly headed outside. The sight of Keisha behind the wheel of the new sports car stunned them momentarily.

"Damn! This car is the business," Sherrie said.

"You want it? You can have it." Keisha stared straight ahead, tears brimming in her eyes.

"Keisha, you're not going to give this bitch a forty-thousand-dollar car," Tameka said. "I know you feel like your world is ending, but I promise you, it will get better. Now, let's go get that degree you worked so hard for."

"I don't feel like it, Tameka. I just want to ball up in the corner and die."

"Quit talking like that. Life is unfair. The ones you love are the ones who hurt you the most. But, what don't kill you makes you stronger. Now, let's go get your diploma!"

"Tameka, I know you mean well, but I can't. How can I put a smile on my face and walk across the stage when it hurts so much?"

"Listen, Keisha, there is a bachelor's degree in marketing and advertising waiting on you. You worked your ass off for that degree, so you're gonna walk across that stage and make your father proud. Now, move the hell over and let's go. I'm driving, your vision's a little impaired right now."

A small smile crept onto Keisha's face. "You just want to get behind the wheel," she said, getting out the car and walking around to the passenger side.

"Yes, I do," Tameka said, sliding behind the wheel,

The three of them laughed as they drove away.

The commencement ceremony was over by the time Keisha arrived at the college. She got a chance to say good-bye to some of her professors, but all of her classmates were gone except one.

"Congratulations, Ms. Lee. I hope this won't be the last time that we see each other."

Sherman looked like a model and had the height and physique of an NBA player. His smooth dark skin, chestnut brown eyes, and goatee complemented his perfectly structured face and even white teeth. Those features, combined with his taper-cut, wavy black hair, made him easy on the eyes. He handed Keisha a card and a fragrant bouquet of roses.

"I'm sorry, I don't have anything for you," she said, admiring her flowers.

"That's a'ight, Miss Lady. I didn't expect anything. Remember, expectation is the only thing that hurts us in life." He flashed a smile. "I have to go. My family is waiting for me. I wrote my number on the card. Call me when you get a chance." He kissed her on the cheek and walked away.

"Damn, girl! He is fine. Who the hell is that?" Tameka and Sherrie stared after him.

"That's Sherman. He was in a couple of my classes."

"Oooooh, he has it bad for you," Sherrie said.

Keisha rolled her eyes. "Girl, I'm done with men."

Tameka and Sherrie looked at each other, then looked at her, their eyebrows raised.

"Y'all crazy." She laughed. "I'm not going to women. I just need time to myself. Let's go get something to eat."

"What do you wanna eat?" Sherrie asked, picking a rose from Keisha's bouquet and sniffing it. "He likes you, Keisha. It's not every day that a man buys a girl he's not sleeping with a dozen roses and keeps his family waiting so he can give 'em to her."

"Whatever. You're reading too much into it. He's cool peeps, nothing more than that. Back to your question, I want a good, home-cooked meal," Keisha said, rubbing her stomach.

"MacArthur's it is," Sherry said

"First, let's go change. I want to change into something more comfortable. This dress is too tight," Tameka complained.

"I told you to get your size. You always squeezing your big butt into something too small," Sherrie said.

"Shut up. It's not too small, I just can't move around like I want to.

"Yeah, whatever." Tameka waved a hand at Sherrie as if to say I don't want to hear it.

"My dress is too dressy to be dining in the hood," Keisha said. "Damn, I don't have anything else. All my clothes are at the house and I can't go back there."

"Well, let's go buy you something. My treat," Tameka said.

"It's cool, I got it. A bitch did leave with a stash."

"Hell, in that case, buy me something." Tameka laughed.

Keisha pulled a wad of money out of her purse. "No problem. Let's go somewhere close by. I don't feel like dealing with the hassle downtown. Wait, I know the perfect spot." She grabbed her phone out of her purse and started dialing. "Hello, Sincere, this is Keisha. Clear the store out. My girls and I are coming through and I really don't feel like being bothered with the hoodrats." She listened to the answer on the other end of the line and then hung up. "Let's go," she said, leading Tameka and Sherrie to the car.

Sincere didn't hesitate to clean house. She knew that Keisha would spend more money in one day than all those chicks would spend together in a year.

Sincere Apparel was the hottest boutique on Chicago's Southside. She supplied all the ballers' chicks with top-of-the-line apparel at a discounted price. Stepping into the store, shoppers instantly forget that they are in the hood. The decor of the store was similar to those featured in upscale magazines.

Upon entering, customers step into the illusion that they are rich, important, and persons of influence. A large crystal chandelier hung in the middle of the ceiling and Versace gold and white curtains draped across the display window. In the lounge area across from the fitting room sat four antique high-back, royalty-inspired, hand-carved chairs and behind the glass counter stood a ten-foot-tall and five-foot-wide, custom-built waterfall. Clothing and jewelry displays were subtle, but eye-catching.

The owner's style was versatile. On any given day of the week, she could be seen rocking looks ranging from high-end, Old Hollywood glam style to business to an edgy B-girl-from-around-the-way. Throughout the store, she'd hung pictures of iconic women, both past and present, whose fashion sense she admired—Dianne Carroll, Eartha Kitt, Diana Ross, Lena Horne, Jada Pinkett-Smith, Mary J. Blige, Beyoncé, and Rihanna.

"Damn, girl, you got it like that?" Sherrie asked as the trio sped down the highway.

"Yeah, Dino spends a lot of money with Sincere. Hell, you can say that she's my personal shopper. Even when I don't get clothes from her boutique, she shops for me at other stores."

"She does have an eye for fashion. She be G'd from head to toe every time I see her," Sherrie said.

They arrived at the store and Keisha pulled around to the back. She honked the horn and Sincere came to the door and waved for them to come in.

"Nice car, graduation gift?" she asked.

"Graduation and forgive-me-for-I-have-sinned gift," Keisha replied.

They laughed and hugged. Sincere acknowledged Tameka and Sherrie, then led the three girl into the store.

"Sincere, today I want something very provocative. I want it to hug my hips, boost my breasts, and show off my long legs," Keisha said.

"I got the perfect outfits for you already laid out, but don't tell that man of yours that you got it from me."

"I won't."

"I'm serious. I don't want to hear that fool's mouth."

"Keep it real. You don't want him to stop spending those Benjamin's with you."

"That too," Sincere said, laughing.

Although she was ten years older, the boutique owner and Keisha had always been cool with each other. Dino, who Sincere had gone to high school with, had introduced the two of them and they'd taken to each other instantly. Sincere knew the hell he was putting the younger girl through. She'd gone through the same problems with her ex before he'd gotten killed.

"My girls need a fit too. Pick them out the hottest shit you got, but don't let my bill go over twenty-five hundred."

Sherrie and Tameka grinned and high-fived each other. They were honored to have Sincere style them. They admired her style.

Sincere looked at Sherrie and Tameka, assessing their sizes. "You both are about a size eight, correct?"

Sherrie was impressed. "Yeah, we are. You're good."

Sincere gave her a wink and a smile and started gathering items for them. "I got you covered. Dino must be out of town," she commented to Keisha.

"Yes, he is."

"In that case, let me pull out some bubbly."

Keisha frowned. "I can't drink. I haven't eaten all day."

"I'll order us a pizza. I'll go get the number to Italian Fiesta." Sincere headed toward her office.

After the pizza was delivered, Sincere untied the drapes and allowed them to fall closed so no one could see inside the store. She put a closed sign in the window and they talked, ate, and drank.

Hours passed and the sun went down. The ladies talked about everything from food to fashion and caught up on all the neighborhood and celebrity gossip.

"We've been in here all day." Tameka said.

"Yeah, it's time for me to lock up and head home. I have a busy day ahead of me tomorrow," Sincere said as she started to clean up the pizza box and champagne bottles. "Enjoy y'all outfits and congratulations, Keisha. Oh, before I forget, I got something for you."

She gave Keisha a box wrapped in metallic pink wrapping with a purple satin bow.

"You shouldn't have," Keisha said.

"You know I had to give my favorite customer and friend something on her special day."

Keisha's eyes watered, not because of the gift, but from being reminded of just how *special* her day had begun.

"Don't cry, girl. It's not that expensive of a gift,"

Sincere teased.

"Thank you, Sincere. For everything—the long talks, the knowledge, and the wisdom that you've shared with me over the years. You've been like a big sister to me."

"You're welcome, baby. I'd do anything for you, anything. All you have to do is ask." Sincere knew that Keisha was holding something in. She also knew that Keisha would talk to her about it in her own time.

"I really wanted some MacArthur's," Tameka announced as they left.

"I did too. I want some of their banana pudding," Keisha said.

"Well, let's ride out there," Sherrie suggested. "They close at eight, it's just seven-thirty. I'm sure we can make it."

Traffic was hectic. They arrived five minutes too late.

"Since we over here, let's ride down to the Circle," Sherrie said.

"The Circle? What is that?" Keisha asked.

"Damn. I forgot Dino had you under lock and key like a damned prisoner. It's like Washington Park. People go there and hang out," Tameka explained. "You wanna go?"

"Yeah, anything to keep my mind occupied."

They drove to the Circle and found it was packed. Half-naked girls sat on top of cars and guys flexed their muscles, some shirtless and others in white tanks, doing their best to impersonate a street baller image,

"This shit is crazy. Look at the buffet of dudes," Keisha said, shaking off her funk.

"I know, right?" Tameka said, applying lip-gloss and checking herself out in the mirror.

"Park so we can get out and walk," Sherrie said.

Keisha found a space and they all got out. They walked past a group of guys leaning on a black Range Rover and the fellas started yelling, whispering, and waving for them to come over.

"What's up, ma? Can I get your number?" one called out.

Damn, all y'all look good," said another.

"I like this attention," Sherrie said as she smiled and waved back at the guys.

A dude with texturized curly hair and his shirt half-way open, showing his chiseled chest, walked up to Tameka and asked for her number.

She looked him up and down and said, "You didn't even ask me my name."

"I already know it."

"What is it?"

"Beautiful."

"What?"

"If that's not your name, it should be."

Keisha and Sherrie looked at each other and rolled their eyes, telegraphing to each other that they knew he was full of shit.

"No, seriously," he said, "My name is June. What's yours?"

"It's Tameka."

Keisha and Sherrie walked away and left Tameka to talk to her new friend.

"These West Side guys sure come on strong, don't they?" Sherrie said.

"Yeah, with that weak-ass line. But he does look good. He looks a little like Ginuwine."

Sherrie and Keisha walked the Circle twice, trying to see if someone caught their eye.

"This is boring and I'm tired of walking," Keisha said. "Let's go get Tameka and bounce."

After going back for Tameka, they walked toward the car. On the way, Keisha heard someone call her name. She stopped and looked around, but she didn't recognize anyone.

"Hey, what's up stranger? Long time, no see," a six-foot-two, dark-skinned guy said as he approached them. He was extremely attractive and had a body built like a pro athlete—strong and masculine. They could see the ripples in his stomach through his fitted, white tank. On his left arm was the face of a woman with the words "Gone but never forgotten, RIP Mom." Long, thick dread-locks were neatly braided back into a ponytail, comple-menting his manicured, chin-strip facial hair.

The three girls stared. He chuckled, knowing the im-pact his looks had on women.

Keisha shook her head and focused on his face, try-ing to remember him. She looked up into his dark brown eyes, but drew a blank. "I'm sorry, do I know you?" she asked.

"Yeah, girl, you know me," he said in his deep voice. "I'm yo' cousin, Dre. Andre... Ray's son."

Keisha stared him up and down again, this time

without admiration. *The son of my father's killer,* she thought. *Can this day get any worse?*

"Why you looking at me like that? You don't believe me? I know you not still checking me out; I just told you I'm your cousin. You know that's considered incest and illegal in some states," he said, joking. "But, yo' girls still welcome to admire." He rubbed his chin, his eyes taking in Sherrie's curves.

Embarrassed by what he said and uncomfortable with his stare, Sherrie looked away.

Keisha shrugged. "No, it isn't that. I'm not having a good day. So, how's your father?" she asked nonchalantly, praying her uncle was dead, strung out on drugs, or homeless somewhere.

"I couldn't tell you. To be honest, I don't fuck with him. He was never a father to me or J.R. Your dad was more of a father to us."

"How did you remember me?" she asked, warming to him since he told her he didn't associate with his father.

"How could I forget you? We lived with y'all for about a year after my mom died. Are you still a spoiled ass? How's your mom? You look just like her by the way. That's how I really recognized you," he explained.

"My mom is doing fine. I remember you now. You used to take my Barbie doll heads and hide them."

"That would be me," he said with a laugh.

Keisha smiled. "Well, we're about to leave and head back south. It was nice seeing you."

"Wait, cuz. Give me yo' number and I'll call you tomorrow. We can go to lunch and catch up. I know my brother will be happy to see you."

Just as Andre pulled out his phone, a short, big booty,

light-skinned girl sipping something from a plastic cup walked over. She wore short shorts that her butt cheeks hung from underneath and a cut-up shirt that showed her lacy pink bra. She stood between Andre and Keisha with her back to Keisha and pointed a finger in his face.

"Every time I turn my back, you all up in some bitch face. You gone make me catch a murda out here." She turned around and rolled her eyes at Keisha.

"Excuse me?" Keisha said. "Who are you calling a bitch? I know you couldn't possibly be speaking of me. Don't let my appearance fool your thirsty-looking ass. You about to get fuck up out of here."

Andre grabbed the girl by the back of her neck, causing her lose her grip on her drink. "Girl, don't you ever disrespect my cousin like that again."

The girl's eyes widened. "I'm sorry, baby, I didn't know she fam." Andre let her go and she turned to Keisha. Apologizing, she tried to hug her, but Keisha stepped back.

"My fault, cuz. He's the biggest fish out here and you know these bitches out here paper chasin'. No harm intended. I'm Tabitha," she said pronouncing every syllable in her name and chewing gum with her mouth open. She tried again to give Keisha a hug, but Keisha moved away again, this time giving her a look that could kill.

The idea of her long lost cousin being a "big fish" interested Keisha. Deciding he could be beneficial to her, she gave him her number.

"I'll call you tomorrow, cuz," Andre said before turning his attention to Tabitha. "Come on. You lucky I love yo' crazy ass." He grabbed her and walked off hugging her hips and squeezing her ass.

"Daddy, you know I have to protect my property,"

she said.

"Damn, these chicks out here are crazy," Sherrie said, watching them leave.

"Not crazier than the ones out south," Tameka said. "Maybe just a little bolder."

"Yeah, but she was about to get her ass kicked Southside style," Keisha said.

They three gave each other a high-five and left.

On the ride home, no one talked much. They dropped Sherrie off, then Keisha and Tameka headed to Tameka's house. Keisha had decided to stay with her for a couple of days until she figured out new living arrangements.

They tiptoed in the house so they wouldn't awaken Tameka's mom and went into Tameka's room. Keisha noticed a poster on the wall that stopped her in her tracks.

"Girl, I can't believe you still have this poster from *The Last Dragon* hanging on your wall. How old are you again?" She laughed.

"Ha, ha, twenty-two just like you. Laugh all you want, I still plan on becoming Mrs. Tameka Guarriello one day."

"Tameka, he is old as dirt! You do know that, right? More than likely, he doesn't look the same. Hell, the movie was more than eight years old when we saw it. We were around ten and he had to be in his late twenties in the movie. He has to be close to fifty by now."

"I don't care. You know I like those pretty boys. You see I still have my Al B. Sure poster too." She pointed to it and they both fell on the bed, laughing hysterically.

"So, what's up with the guy at the park? What is he on?" Keisha asked after she caught her breath.

"He seems cool. No kids, he claims. He say he own a few properties. I'm going to see what's really good with him though."

"Yes, he most definitely is your type—pretty boy to the fullest."

"And you know this *man,*" Tameka said in her Chris Tucker voice, slipping on her nightgown and passing Keisha one.

Once settled in bed, Keisha had difficulty falling asleep. Her mind wouldn't let her. She kept replaying the scene of her mom and Dino in bed together.

She choked back tears, but couldn't suppress her sobbing. Tameka woke up when she heard the crying. She rolled over and looked at her best friend. "Keisha, girl, you have to get some sleep."

"I can't. I keep picturing them together." She shook her head as if to shake the image out of her head. "Do you think Dino is going to get out?"

"I don't know. How much drugs was it?"

"Not much."

"It all depends on his parole officer and his lawyer."

"His lawyer?" Keisha asked. She hadn't even thought about a lawyer.

"Yeah, if his lawyer is good, he'll come up with a way to get him off."

"Why hasn't he called yet? He knows, doesn't he?" Keisha asked nervously. She started to think her plan wouldn't work. What if Dino heard her when she was in the kitchen? What if he saw her hiding in the bushes?

Fearful thoughts and questions ran through her head.

"No, he's still going through the process. He'll call you tomorrow, probably first thing in the morning. I went through the same thing with my ex when he got locked up and I've seen it a million times before with guys on the block. He doesn't know. He'd never think that you'd do something like that. Now, get some sleep. You need it."

"I can't believe my mom would do that to me. This was supposed to be the one of the happiest days of my life."

"Keisha, your mother is on drugs. She's not herself. She didn't do it; the drugs did it. Remember that. Don't hate your mother, help her get some help. Dino took advantage of her. He probably told her that he'd give her an unlimited supply if she slept with him."

"It's easy for someone to say the drugs made them do it. *Your* mother is on drugs. Do you think she'd ever do something like that to you?"

"My mom's not on drugs any more. She drinks, though. And I honestly don't know what she'd do. I can't seem keep a man long enough to find out, so, I'll probably never know," Tameka said, making Keisha laugh. "Now, take your ass to sleep. Goodnight."

"Goodnight, Tameka."

Chapter 3

*K*eisha awoke to the distinctive smell of bacon. She gagged from the unpleasant scent. She hadn't eaten pork in seven years. Dino didn't believe in eating "swine" as he called it.

"So, you finally decided to wake up," Tameka said. A plate of pancakes, eggs, and bacon sat on the table in front of her.

"What time is it?" Keisha asked, sitting down and taking a piece of pancake off Tameka's plate.

"Noon."

"Noon? I never sleep this late."

"I do all the time. Especially when I don't have someone in my room crying and then snoring all night."

"I'm sorry about the crying, but your ass is lying about the snoring."

Before Tameka could respond, her mother, Jennifer, walked into the kitchen. The faded, over-sized caftan she wore took nothing away from her beauty. Her smooth, dark skin, small waist, and double-D breasts still commanded attention. Her signature pixie cut showed off her honey-colored eyes.

"Hey baby, I thought I heard your voice last night. Come over here and give your godmomma a hug. I haven't seen you in a while. Tell Dino that you still have family in the city and we'd like to see you from time to time. I know you're hungry, you want me to fix you something?"

"Yes, I am. I'll take everything but the bacon, Momma J. I don't eat pork or beef," Keisha said, sitting back down.

"I should've known that. I'll see if I can find some turkey for you."

"Thank you, Momma J."

"Baby, I'm so proud of you. How does it feel to be a college graduate?"

"It feels the same, I guess." Keisha shrugged.

"Wish I could've been there to see you walk across the stage."

"I wish I could've been there too," Keisha mumbled.

"What did you say, baby?"

"Oh, I said I'm sorry I didn't have enough tickets for you."

"That's all right. I know your mother, your man, and your godsisters are your first priority."

"It's not like that. You're important to me. I love you just the same."

"I know you do, baby. I'm just kidding with you. So how is that crazy-ass mother of yours?"

Keisha wanted to say, "That bitch really is crazy. I caught her sleazy ass in the bed with my man." But she smiled instead and said, "She's doing fine. Same ole', same ole'."

Jennifer stopped digging in the freezer and turned to

looked at Keisha. "Are you sure? You know I can always tell when you're lying."

"No, she's fine." Keisha tried to sound upbeat.

"Mom, quit pestering her," Tameka intervened.

"Girl, shut the hell up and go get my glass out of my room. Ain't nobody pestering her. I'm surprised you even know what that word means."

Tameka left the kitchen, rolling her eyes.

"Keisha, you know I will always love your mother, but sometimes love isn't enough to stay in any relationship," Jennifer said.

"Momma J, can I ask you a question?"

"Ask away."

"What happened between you and my mother?"

"Some things, regardless of how old a child gets, should remain between elders."

"I don't understand, though. You guys were so close. How can y'all act like the other doesn't even exist?"

"What can I say? Shit happens."

"I can't imagine life without Tameka and Sherrie. I'd hurt someone over them."

"And you don't have to. You girls have been friends since you were three. I won't let you girls break up. True friends are hard to find these days. Now that's enough of this sad talk. When I get my check on the first, I'm gonna buy you something."

"You don't have to."

"I know I don't, but I am. You're my godbaby. I love you just like you my own child. It wouldn't feel right if I didn't. And I want you to talk to Tameka about going back to school. I don't want her to be like me, depending on the government or a man to take care of her."

"I'll try. You know how stubborn she is."

"Who are you telling?" Jennifer said lighting up a cigarette.

"I don't need anybody to talk to me about school," Tameka said, re-entering the kitchen. She handed her mother her morning glass of liquor. "Mom, school isn't for everyone."

"But, Tameka, you at least need a GED."

Tameka rolled her eyes. She had dropped out of school after her eighth grade graduation because she didn't like being told what to do. She had always been rebellious and thought she knew everything. In her opinion, a person without a degree could make just as much money as a person with one. The hustlers she knew made more money working three-hour shifts than the average person working nine to five.

"I'm going to be an entrepreneur," she said proudly.

Her mother sighed and shook her head. "Entrepreneurs need an education, Tameka."

"Look at P. Diddy and Russell Simmons. They don't have college degrees."

"But they went to college, Tameka," Keisha said.

"Well, that's them, I'm me. Besides, isn't our rent paid every month? Don't we keep food in the fridge and clothes on our backs?"

"Girl, you sound stupid. You should always want more for yourself. Don't just be content with what you have," Keisha argued.

"That's easy for you to say. Mom, have you seen her

new car?"

Keisha looked at Tameka and shook her head. She opened her mouth to speak again, but her phone rang before she could say anything. Jumping up, she ran to Tameka's room, almost tripping over the long phone cord lying across the floor in the hallway. *Haven't they heard of cordless?* she thought.

When she made it to the room, her phone had stopped ringing. Checking the caller ID, she saw that it was a private call. She knew it had to be Dino.

The phone rang again and she got nervous, her stomach knotting up. She was anxious and scared at the same time. "Tameka, come here. Hurry, I think it's him."

"Let me see," Tameka said, walking into the room. "How do you know that's him? It says 'Private.'"

"I know because nobody calls my phone from a private number. What should I do?"

"Hurry up and answer before it goes to voicemail."

"But, I'm scared."

"Don't be. Sound concern and worried. Men love that shit."

Keisha took a deep breath and prepared herself to get into character. "Okay," she said, then answered the phone. "Hello?"

"Hello," a male voice said on the other end.

"Who is this?" Keisha asked, already knowing the answer.

"Who the fuck you think this is?" Dino growled.

"Dino, where are you? And why are you calling me private? I went home and couldn't get in. There was a big padlock on the front and back door," she said, embellishing. "Where's my mother and why didn't either of you come to my graduation? That's how you both do me, huh?"

Tameka nodded, showing her approval of Keisha's Academy Award-worthy performance.

"Keisha, I'm in jail," Dino said, clearly agitated.

"What do you mean you're in jail? What happened? Whose phone are you on?"

"Your dope fiend-ass momma set me up."

"What? What did you say?"

"You heard me."

Keisha held the phone and said nothing.

Dino drew in a deep breath. He knew he wasn't in a position to talk to her like that. Not when he needed her more than ever. He didn't want to piss her off when he needed her help, so he changed his tone.

"I'm sorry, baby. I didn't mean for it to come out like that. I can't think straight in this place. You know I hate being locked up. I didn't mean what I said. My man from the block is a C.O. here. I'm using his phone. All I know is that I was upstairs in the shower when the cops came busting in the door. They snatched me out the shower, threw me on the floor, and told me I was under arrest."

"Where was my mother?"

"She was downstairs somewhere," he lied.

"So what did they do to her? And why do you think she set you up?"

"She was the only other person there. I don't feel like talking about that shit right now. Where did you sleep last night?" he asked, changing the subject.

"At Tameka's," Keisha said, rolling her eyes.

"I figured that. Keisha, listen, I need you to go to the house and do exactly what I say, then contact my lawyer. I tried calling him, but didn't get an answer. The voice-mail keep picking up. They must be closed for the holiday and I don't know his cell number by heart. You need to get in the house. Our future depends on it. I need you to get my CD collection."

You mean your *future*, Keisha thought. "CDs?" she said, trying to figure out what he was talking about.

"Yeah, the ones I told you were *sentimental* to me," he said. "When you get in the house, push the refrigerator off the wall, count three tiles from away the wall, and use a screwdriver to lift that tile up. You'll see a string; pull it. The bag you'll see is heavy, so be careful not to rip it. Take one of the CDs to my lawyer, then go rent a room downtown and stay there until I get out. Don't call anybody from the room. *Nobody.* That includes Tameka and Sherrie."

"Why do I have to lock myself up in a room for three days? It's the weekend and Monday is a holiday. You won't go to court until Tuesday. Why can't I just stay here at Tameka's?"

"Baby, it's for your own good."

Keisha knew that staying in a hotel wasn't for her safety; she had nothing to fear. It was for Dino to know her exact whereabouts and keep her off the block and away from Sherrie. He wasn't too fond of Sherrie and the last thing he wanted was her friend planting negative seeds about him in Keisha's head.

"Okay, Dino" She sighed. "But how will I find out about my mother?" she asked.

"When I come home, I'll have my lawyer look into it. I'll call you later to see if you got the CDs. Don't go in any other room except the kitchen. They probably dusted for prints."

"Is that it?"

"Yeah, that's it. Be careful, baby. I love you," Dino said. "Did you hear me," he bellowed when she said nothing. "I said I love you."

Keisha ground her teeth and squeezed her hand into a fist. "I love you too."

"Okay, baby. I'll call you in a couple hours."

"I'll wait on your call." She hung up and started getting dressed. "Tameka, I gotta go."

"Wait, I'm going with you. What did he say?" Tameka asked.

"He lied about everything."

"So, does he think it's you?"

"No, he blames my mother."

"What?" Her friend's mouth dropped open.

"That's exactly what I thought. He really doesn't think I'm capable of doing shit."

"That's a good thing."

"I guess," Keisha said, pulling on her jeans.

Thirty minutes later, the two were headed to Keisha's house. When they turned onto the tree-lined street Keisha lived on, Tameka gaped at the big, beautiful houses. She saw people of different ethnicities jogging and conversing with each other in a friendly manner. In her neighborhood, the only time she saw a white person with a black one is when they were getting high, selling something, a white police officer beating or harassing a black person, or a white girl fucking the neighborhood biggest dealer.

"Keisha, I can't believe you live out here. It's so quiet and beautiful," she said.

"I know. It took me a long time to get used to the peace. Hell, I was used to hearing gunshots at night before I went to sleep and first thing when I woke up." Keisha look over at Tameka, feeling guilty. "You know I would've invited you and Sherrie over, but Dino wasn't having it."

"Girl, I'm not tripping. And you're not lying about the gunshots."

Keisha drove around to the back of the house and parked.

"Damn, how am I'm going to get in?" she wondered aloud. "I can't risk going in the front and somebody seeing me."

"What about that window. What room is that?" Tameka asked.

"The kitchen. I need a ladder."

She went to the garage and got the ladder. Keisha climbed in first, then Tameka.

"Damn, Keisha," Tameka said, looking around the spacious kitchen. "This is a *MTV Cribs*-crib. I didn't know you were living like this. Is it cool if I look around?"

"Go ahead. Knock yourself out."

Tameka stepped into the living room and her feet sank into the plush, white carpet. Looking down, she could no longer see her all-white Air Force Ones. She was impressed by the beauty and elegance of the room. She ran her fingers over the carved accents on the beige, kidney-shaped, Italian leather sofa chaise and glanced approvingly at the wall-to-wall mirrors and marble coffee table.

Over the mantel, she noted an oversized picture in a

Bourlet frame. In the photo, Dino, wearing a black suit, sat in a regal armchair holding a cigar in his left hand. His right arm lay on the armrest, his ten-carat pinky ring shining. Standing beside him, Keisha wore a red, off-the-shoulder, split-front, floor-length evening dress. Her hair was pulled to one side in loose curls, displaying her sparkling diamond earrings and necklace set.

"They sure look good together. Too bad he's a jackass, " Tameka said out loud. Intrigued by the living space, she went from room to room, finding each one better than the last. Upstairs, she was surprised to find that one room she entered had been converted into a walk-in closet like the ones at Ikea. One side was full of shoes; the other side held leather and fur coats. A jewelry display table sat in the center. *I can't believe the cops didn't take this shit. The cops out here must really be different from the city cops.*

"Tameka!" Keisha called. "Come here."

"Here I come," Tameka said, walking down the stairs.

"Help me pull this."

Tameka enter the kitchen and saw Keisha on the floor struggling to pull something from underneath the tiles. "What the hell is in there? A body?"

"I'm not exactly sure."

It took all their strength to pull the bag up. Keisha cautiously opened it, looked inside, and smiled. She reached in and pulled out a stack of money. She fanned through it, then pulled out more stacks—twenties, fifties, and hundreds. She and Tameka couldn't believe their eyes.

"This muthafucka is loaded," Tameka said.

"I knew he had money, but not like this. I should take it all and run. His bitch ass doesn't deserve a dime. This'll be payback for all the torture he put me through."

Keisha's eyes lit up as she thought of what she could do with the money and how she could truly escape Dino. He'd feel stupid for trusting her with so much cash after years of beating and belittling her.

She remembered his words—"Don't go in any other room except the kitchen. They probably dusted for prints." *Dust for prints, I live here, a course they'll find my prints. I know exactly why he doesn't want me to go in any other room,* she thought.

Tameka shook Keisha, bringing her back to reality. "Where would you go?" she asked, shocked that Keisha would consider stealing Dino's money.

"Paris."

"Bitch, get serious. You can't speak a lick of French and you don't know nobody in Paris. Plus, you don't want him to put a price on your head."

"I know, but it sure sounds good. I'm going to take this money, If not all, half. He owes me this. Let's go." Keisha stuffed the money back in the bag.

"What about your clothes?" Tameka asked.

"I'll buy some more. Why? You want 'em?"

"No, I just thought you might want your furs, leather, and jewelry."

"I don't want anything in this house. This stuff only reminds me of all the terrible things that happened to me. This is the house of horror. I wish I could do a Left Eye to this muthafucka," Keisha said, looking around in disgust.

"Let's bounce, Keisha, before you act on that crazy idea. How much money do you think this is?"

"Hell, more than I'll probably make in ten years trying to make an honest living off my degree."

They rushed to the car, put the bag in the trunk, and drove off. Keisha's phone rang just as she turned out of the subdivision.

"Who is this 773-555-2275?" she asked.

"You want me to answer?" Tameka said.

"No, I got it." She took a breath and answered. "Hello."

"Hey, what's up, cuz?"

She recognized the voice. "Nothing much. What's up with you, Andre?"

"What's wrong? You sound on edge."

"No, I'm cool. I was just trying to figure out whose number this was. So what's up?"

"Let me know if you got some drama you need your big cousin to take care for you. We been apart, but blood is blood. And I'll do anything to protect my uncle Chico's baby girl. Ya, hear me?"

"Yes, I do and thank you. That's nice to know."

"I'm calling to see if you still gonna meet us for lunch?"

Keisha look at the clock on the dashboard. "Lunch? It's three o'clock."

"Call it what you want. Lunch, early dinner, it's all eating—"

"I'm kind of busy for the next few days," Keisha said, interrupting him. "I won't be free until Tuesday."

"Tuesday? Today is Friday. What the hell you gon' be doing that'll keep you tied up until next week? I need to be a part of that 'cause it must be some money involved."

"Not anything particular. I just have some personal

business to take care of. I'll call you Tuesday and we'll do lunch. My treat."

"A'ight. Don't fake me out, cousin. I really want to kick it with you. It'll be nice having family around for a change."

"I feel you. I'll call you. I promise."

"Peace."

"So, why won't you kick it with your cousin?" Tameka asked when Keisha hung up. "He seems cool."

"I am, but Dino wants me to go stay in a hotel until he gets out."

"Are you serious? Keisha, you know you my girl and I'll never judge you, but you gotta stop letting him run your life. He's controlling you from behind bars. That don't make no damn sense. Why should you go lock yourself up 'cause he is? You need to stop putting yourself through this shit. You have your degree now. Isn't that what you claim you were waiting for to leave his ass?"

Keisha sighed heavily. She didn't like what Tameka was saying, but she knew it was true, so she didn't argue. They finished the ride in silence, Tameka staring out her window as Keisha drove past abandoned and condemned buildings leading into Tameka's neighborhood. Barefoot children pushed each other in shopping carts, darting in front of traffic.

When Keisha parked in front of Tameka's house, Tameka hopped out and started walking towards her door, narrowly avoiding being hit by a little boy cutting across the unkempt grass on his bike.

Keisha called her name. "Tameka, hold up," she said, getting out of the car and catching up with her. "I'm not mad at you. We always tell each other the truth. Sometimes it's hard hearing reality. I promise you a change is in the works."

"Keisha, don't do something stupid that's gonna get you killed."

"I'm not. I'll call you after I check in."

"A'ight, make sure you call me *immediately* after you check in. Sherrie and I will come down and keep you company."

"I will."

They hugged before Keisha got back in her car and drove off.

Chapter 4

*D*riving north on Lake Shore Drive with her window down and letting the cool breeze flow through her hair, Keisha knew exactly where she would stay—The Ritz-Carlton.

I deserve nothing but the best if I'm going to be locked up for four days, Keisha thought as she pulled up to the valet.

"Do you have any luggage?" the young man asked as he opened the door for her.

"Yes, but I'll get it." She had trouble lifting the bag out the car.

"Let me help you, Miss."

"Okay, thank you." Keisha tipped him fifty dollars. She knew the bigger the tip, the better they'd treat your ride and the less chance they'd steal out of it.

She entered the hotel, her four-inch heels clicking against the marble floor, and looked in awe at the water fountain with a bronze sculpture in the center of the lobby. The hotel had a warm and elegant feel and she was pleased with herself for choosing to stay there. She had read about it in magazines, but it was much more then she had imagined.

"Welcome to the Ritz-Carlton. How may I help you?" the uniformed clerk at the desk asked.

"I'd like a suite with a lakeside view on the top floor," Keisha said.

"I am delighted to help you. Let me check and see what we have available, Mrs...?."

"No, it's *Ms*. Lee."

"Will you need two keys or one?"

"One, thank you."

"We have the Deluxe Lake View Suite with a king-sized bed available."

"That will be fine."

"How many nights will you be staying with us?"

"Four," she said, getting an extra night to be on the safe side.

"Okay, four nights, five days, the total will be $3,652. Will you be putting that on a credit card today?"

"No, I'll pay with cash."

After paying, Keisha got the key and directions to her room and headed toward the elevator. *Even the scent in here is different; it smells rich.*

Inside the elevator, she looked up and saw a large crystal chandelier in the ceiling.

I could get used to this, she thought.

Entering her suite, she went through the double French doors leading from the living area and straight into the bedroom. Opening the bag, she pulled out the money, making rows of stacks on the bed. Then she sat and counted it all, bill by bill. It took her an hour and a half to count it three times. She couldn't believe she had so much money at her disposal.

While putting the money back into the bag, her stomach started to growl, reminding her that she hadn't eaten all day. She scanned the room service menu and called in an order. While waiting for the delivery, she ran bath water in the oversized jet stream tub. Once undressed, she turned on the radio and then stepped into the bubble-filled Jacuzzi. The torture from two nights ago was starting to take its toll and the water soothed her aching body. Just as she closed her eyes to relax, her cell phone rang. She knew it was either Dino or Tameka. She had forgotten to call Tameka like she had promised.

"Hello?"

"Hey, baby, did you do what I asked?" It was Dino.

"Yes, I did."

"That's what's up. I knew I could count on you. Are you okay?"

"Yes, I'm at the hotel."

"Which one?"

"The Ritz-Carlton"

"The Ritz? Why that one? Aren't the rooms about a stack a night?"

"Yes, but you told me you wanted me safe. Hell, Oprah Winfrey lived in the condos upstairs from here for years. How much safer can I get? Besides, what guy do you know personally that will pay this amount a night for a one night stand?"

"True dat, but you just wanted to splurge."

"Well, if I got to be locked up in this room for four long days, I need it to be comfortable. You should see this suite."

"Whatever, man. Did you call my lawyer?"

"Yeah, but I didn't get an answer. I left a message for him to call me back."

There was a knock on the door. "Room service," a voice announced.

"Here I come," she called. She got out the tub, put on a robe, walked through the bedroom to the door and opened it.

"Who's that?" Dino asked.

"Room service, who else?"

"You better not be having a dude coming up there. I know how those five-star hotels be full with athletes on weekends."

"Baby, the only person I'll let in here is MJ."

"MJ, my ass. Keisha, don't get yo' ass kicked."

A tall, good-looking, Middle Eastern man entered the room and set the food on the table. He stared at her and swallowed hard, his Adam's apple bobbing. Stuttering, he bid her a good afternoon and turned to leave.

"How much do I owe you, sir?" Keisha asked with a smile as he headed towards to the door.

"Oh, thank you. I'm so sorry. Silly of me, I assume you charge it to the room," he said in his thick accent. "That will be thirty-two dollars."

Handing him a hundred dollar bill, she told him to keep the change.

"Thank you."

Putting the phone back to her ear, she heard, "Hurry up and get that punk out the room."

Dino had always been insecure when it came to

Keisha. Part of it was because of the way he treated her.

"Dino, stop with the shenanigans. I'm not thinking about him or nobody else. You're the only man I've been with. You think that's going to change overnight because you're locked up? Is that why you be beating my ass? You think I'm a whore? You think by beating me I'll be scared to sleep with someone else? If I wanted anybody besides you, Dino, I would've left you after the first ass whooping. I'm with you because I love you. Not for your money or cause I'm scared. What part of that don't you understand?"

"Keisha, baby I'm sorry. I never meant to insinuate that you're a ho. You're my lady, my love, my life, and one day you'll be my wife. I'll kill for you. Sometimes I let my jealousy and ego get in the way of showing how I truly feel about you, but, baby, I'll die for you," Dino said, sounding sincere.

Keisha's eyes filled with tears. She knew everything he'd just said to her was true and most of what she'd said was a lie. She would never get past him sleeping with her mother and she *was* only with him for shelter and his money. She had stopped loving him a long time ago.

Keisha had met Dino when she was a freshman in high school. He used to come to Keisha's school, stunting and flirting with the young girls. She'd heard of a few girls who had actually slept with him. The rumor was that if you saw a girl get in his car and the next day she came to school wearing new sneakers and her nails and hair were done, she had given up the nookie. He also had a reputation as a women beater.

Keisha had been scared of him at first. He would often drive along beside her, flirting as she walked home from school. He always asked to drive her home and her answer was always the same. "No, I don't ride with strangers."

Persistence outweighs resistance, however, and after months of pursuing, Dino finally won Keisha over, with her mother's approval. His being eight years older than Keisha didn't matter to Isabella, only that he had money and could provide security for her and Keisha.

Their relationship started off like a fairy tale and Keisha never wanted for anything. Dino showered her with gifts. She found it hard to believe the nice, lovable guy she was falling head over heels for was anything like she had heard. After a year and a half, the real Dino—the one she'd been warned about—revealed himself and her life hadn't been the same since. She'd thought that she could change him. She knew the troubles of his childhood and how they had affected him. She didn't want to abandon him like his parents did, so she'd prayed that her love would change him for the better. The more love she showed him, however, the more distant and cold he treated her.

"Baby, I have to go. It's the end of my boy's shift. I'll call you tomorrow, first thing in the morning. But do me a favor before I go."

"What?"

"Go by the mirror."

"What?"

"Just go," he demanded.

Keisha did as instructed. "Okay, I'm by the mirror."

"Lean toward the mirror and kiss it."

"Dino, I'm not kissing a mirror."

"Keisha, please? Do it for me. Don't think of it as kissing a mirror, just close your eyes and picture me. Now, at the count of five…"

"Okay." Keisha leaned toward the mirror and kissed it.

"Goodnight, baby."

"Goodnight, Dino."

Keisha stood staring in the mirror long after he'd hung up, reminiscing about the few good times they had shared. She was in a daze when, suddenly, she heard Ashanti's voice coming through the speakers.

She listened to the lyrics as they described her own situation perfectly—she was a woman who was dying internally. She began to sing along to the words, vocalizing her fear of waking up and believing she wouldn't be around. The song snapped her back to reality. She had to make a change. It was time to escape. The realization felt like the Lord was answering her prayers.

"No more will I allow him to control me. Why am I sitting in this room locked up just because he is?"

She grabbed her phone and called Andre to see if he could meet her at The Cheesecake Factory in an hour. He agreed. Once they hung up, she sent Tameka a text to let her know that she was okay and would call her tomorrow. After dressing in a plain white Dolce & Gabbana, off the shoulder, 100% virgin cotton t-shirt and balloon denim shorts, Gucci signature two-inch heels, and her Tiffany accessories, she pulled her hair up in a sloppy ponytail.

Before leaving, she put as much of the money as she could fit in the safe and then slit the mattress and stuffed the rest in there. Grabbing the key card to the door, she headed out.

When she arrived at the restaurant, Andre wasn't

there yet, so she decided to take a walk and enjoy the downtown scenery.

There's no place in the world like Chicago, she thought.

When she got back, Andre had arrived and was leaning on his car, talking on his cell phone. He saw her approaching and ended the phone called before greeting her with a hug.

"What up, cuz?" he asked.

"What's up with you?" She looked in his car and saw that he had his girl with him. She frowned. "I thought you were bringing your brother with you."

"Yeah, he was busy. He'll hook up with us later. He can't wait to see you. How long can you hang? What time is your curfew?" he joked.

"Funny. My curfew is when the sun rises. Listen, I don't like your girl and I don't want to be around her."

"Chill, cuz, Tabitha cool. But I don't want you uncomfortable, so I'll drop her off."

"I won't be uncomfortable, but she, on the other hand, might be."

Andre opened the back door for Keisha and she got in and sat behind the driver's seat. He got in the car and pulled off.

"Hey, cuz," Tabitha said, turning sideways in her seat to look at Keisha.

Keisha gave her a cold stare and then turned to look out the window.

"Girl, I like that necklace. Did you get it from Rob? He be having all the hot shit."

"Listen, I don't know you, don't like you, and don't care to be around you. So stop the small talk. And FYI, I don't wear knock-offs."

"Cool. I was just trying to keep the peace since Andre plan on being around his long lost cousin. I really don't like or trust *any* bitch around my man anyway, family or not," she said, rolling her neck and looking Keisha up and down before turning around to face the front.

While Tabitha was turning her head and repositioning her body, Keisha reached forward, over the seat and punched her in the side of her face, knocking her earring out of ear and her head into the passenger window. Before the girl could recover, Keisha hit her again.

Andre couldn't believe it. He tried his best to get Keisha off Tabitha with one hand while steering the car with the other. As soon as he could, he pulled over to the side of the road. Before he could do anything, Keisha jumped into the front seat between him and Tabitha and pounded her fist into Tabitha's face repeatedly. The girl tried to fight back, but Keisha had her pinned down.

Finally, he managed to pull Keisha off his girlfriend and out of the car.

"Let me the go. I'm gonna kill that bitch." Keisha huffed. "I told your ass not to let my looks fool you, didn't I, bitch?" Breathing heavily, she paced back and forth behind of the car.

"Cousin, calm down, please. She didn't mean anything by that. You left her no choice but to come back at you like that."

"I told you that I didn't like that bitch. See, I let her slide with the first 'bitch' in the park, but she fucked up with the second one."

At that moment, Tabitha jumped out of the car with a steering wheel club in her hand.

Andre grabbed the metal bar from her hand. "Girl, what the fuck is wrong with you? Get yo' ass back in the car. Y'all gon' stop this bullshit. Keisha, get in the goddamn car."

"I'm not getting in shit with her." Keisha said with her hands on her hips, tapping one foot.

"Keisha, we in the middle of the highway."

"I don't care. I'll call a cab."

"Girl, your little ass is a trip. Give me a second, I'll call you a ride."

He took his phone out of his pocket and she heard him call for someone to come get her.

While he was talking, she walked over to the driver's side-view mirror and started checking her face for marks. Finishing his call, Andre turned and saw her by the car. He rushed over and grabbed her.

"What? Let me go. I'm just checking to make sure I don't have any scratches."

"You're a feisty one. You know you fucked it up for me for later. It'll probably be a week before she gives me some ass," he said, laughing.

"Please, that trick will be sucking you off as soon as y'all get home."

He laughed again. "Where did you learn to throw a punch like that?"

"Don't know. I guess it's in my blood. I did hit her kinda hard," she said, laughing with him.

About fifteen minutes later a car pulled up and a guy jumped out. "So this how we do it?" he said, walking over to them. "A family reunion on the Dan Ryan? What up, cuz? Long time, no see." He grabbed Keisha and hugged her.

"I know, right. I see you lost your baby fat," she said with a smile, remembering how chubby J.R. had been as a kid.

"Yeah, well, you know. I was bound to lose it with all the exercise I'm doing—lifting this chick, that chick—"

"This man is a fool, cuz. You have to excuse him," Andre said, interrupting him.

"It's cool."

Looking at J.R., Keisha could tell that he was a ladies' man. He was very attractive—tall, fair-skinned, hazel eyes, wavy hair, no facial hair, dimples, and slim with white teeth that it seemed he loved to show given how much he was grinning— a pretty boy, gigolo type. He looked like he'd just stepped out of GQ magazine. He was the total opposite of Andre.

"So you out here acting like you're Laila Ali, huh? Let me go see your damage," J.R. said, walking over to Andre's car.

"What the hell you come over here for?" Tabitha snapped.

"I just wanted to make sure you okay."

"I'm fine. It's nothing. She got one up on me, it's cool," she said, rubbing the side of her head.

J.R. put his hands up in surrender. "A'ight, as long as you're straight, ma."

He walked away from the car smiling, holding a fist to his mouth, and grabbing his crotch with his other hand. He put an arm around Keisha and started walking toward his car.

"Come on, cuz, let's go."

"Dre, meet us in Greek town," he called back to his brother.

"I'll meet y'all there in a few."

"Cuz, I'm glad you knocked the hell out that bitch," J.R. said when they got in the car. "I hate her stupid ass. She always calling the cops on my brother for petty shit. She need to be calling them when he be whooping that ass, but no, only when she catch him with another chick."

"Why is he still with her?" Keisha frowned.

"Love. And the bitch is a rider. Let's just say she's a valuable asset. So what you been up to?" he asked, changing the subject.

"Nothing much," she answered. I just graduated with a bachelor's in marketing and advertising."

Looking out the window, she noticed men on the street nodding at J.R. in acknowledgement of his well-maintained '64 convertible, black Pontiac as they drove by. She leaned back, indulging in the comfortable seats in the classic car.

"Congrats! That's a wonderful accomplishment. Are you going back for your master's?"

"I don't know yet."

"You should. Go all the way. There's nothing more threatening in a woman than her brain. Men know that when they step to you, they have to come correct. Where's your man? I know you not single; somebody snatched you up."

"He's locked up."

"For what and how long he been locked up?"

"He just went the other day. I really don't want to talk about it."

"It's cool, I understand. How's your mom? It's unbelievable how much you look like her."

So I constantly hear, she thought as he pulled over and parked outside a restaurant.

"She's cool. Same ole', same ole'," Keisha said, looking out the window to avoid eye contact. Her mother was the last person she wanted to talk about.

"She still be cooking Italian food?"

"Every now and then. She mostly cooks soul food."

"I can't wait to see her. Here comes Andre."

"So you calmed down, Muhammad?" Andre said, reaching into the car and massaging Keisha's shoulders before opening the door.

"Yeah, I'm cool," she said.

"That was fast, bro."

"I know, man. She's mad as hell right now. I'm gonna hear this shit for the next month or so. Man, I'm going to have to go buy her some Louie Vuitton, Tiffany or something." Andre said, laughing while patting his pocket.

So that's a guy thing? Beat her ass and buy a gift. Get caught cheating, buy a piece of expensive jewelry and stay in the house for a couple of days. Make her feel less than human, buy her a car, Keisha thought, leaning on the car and listening.

"Hey, look, I gotta go, J.R. said. "I got this fine ass, super-thick tenderoni waiting on me. Cuz, don't be a stranger. Tell your mother I said hi and I can't wait to see her. Peace, I'm out."

"A'ight I won't," Keisha said. "Peace."

He gunned the engine and peeled off like the police were chasing him.

"You hungry?" Andre asked. "You want something to eat? Hell after a fight like that, you should have a appetite."

"Stop it, silly. But, yes, I'm starving actually."

"Let's go in this restaurant here. They have some good food. Order me a gyro dinner with extra sauce, hot sauce on my fries, and a Coke with no ice. And get whatever you want." He handed her a fifty-dollar bill.

"I'll grab us some seats before it gets full in here." He looked at his cell phone. "In a few minutes, this place is gonna be packed. This is where everybody comes to eat and hang out after the club."

Keisha got in line and Andre went to a table. Before she got to the counter, the door opened and people poured in. Girls walked barefoot with their shoes in hand, their feet aching and swollen from dancing in stilettos for hours. She could barely hear herself think over the noise of the crowd.

After placing their orders, she picked up the drinks and walked over to the small table he'd chosen.

"Andre, I'm sorry about tonight. I've just been going through something and was in a funky mood. I really would've taken my frustration out on anyone. Your girl just happened to be the one. I still don't like her, but I feel terrible about complicating things for you. You didn't deserve that." Keisha said, stirring her straw around in her drink.

When Andre didn't respond, she looked up. "Are you listening to me?" Holding one of the restaurant menus in front of his face, his attention was on something outside. "Andre," she said louder, trying to get his attention.

"Yeah, yeah, it's cool, cuz. Don't sweat it. We all good," he replied, still looking outside.

Looking through the window herself, Keisha didn't see anything but a group of guys across the street. Watching Andre closely, it seemed he was focused on one of the guys in particular. She wondered why Andre was hiding his face and watching the guy. *Is he one of his girlfriend's baby daddies or something?* she thought. *I know he not out here on some punk shit like that.*

Her stomach growled, so she got up and went back to the counter to check on their order. Waiting impatiently while the cashier took his time bagging their food, she was surprised when Andre came from behind her and grabbed her arm, pulling her out of the restaurant.

"Come on, cuz. We gotta go," he said.

"But we haven't eaten yet, and I'm hungry," Keisha whined pulling her arm free.

"I'll get you something else. Let's go," he commanded.

They hopped into his car and sped off. Keisha saw that they were trailing the guy he had been staring at.

"Wh...? Where are we going? Why are you following him?" she asked.

Was he going to jack the guy for his car? Having been a victim of a carjack before, she was nervous. She had only just reconnected with her cousin and really didn't know what he was on. She knew he had money though, so why would he want to jack somebody?

Andre didn't answer Keisha. He followed the car for nearly two miles, keeping a good distance between them. "This nigga is snoozing," he thought.

The other car stopped for a red light and Andre pulled up alongside of him. He knew the other driver wouldn't be able to see him with Keisha sitting in the passenger seat. He saw the man's hand lift in greeting to her.

"Let your seat back," Andre instructed Keisha; screwing a silencer on a gun he'd pulled from underneath his seat.

"What the fuck are you doing? I don't want to be part of this. Take me back to my hotel right now!" Keisha's eyes were wide, watching her cousin.

"You won't. Just let your seat back and relax," he said. The look on his face made her shut up and do as she was told. He pushed the button to roll her window down and blew his horn to get the guy's attention.

The guy looked over, smiling. Andre leaned forward, smiled back at him, and pulled the trigger. The bullet went through the window of the other car and between the guy's eyes. A topless girl sat up from where she'd been leaning over his lap, wiping her mouth and shaking glass out of her hair. She looked at the guy's bloody face and the mess of blood and brain matter all over the front seat and began screaming.

Andre sped off, made a u-turn, and drove away in the opposite direction.

"What the hell did you just do? Oh, my God." Hysterical and panicking, Keisha could barely speak. Unable to control herself, she threw up. This was the first time she'd ever seen anyone get killed.

Andre pulled over into an alley and rushed to her aid.

She jumped out the car, wiping her mouth. "Get the hell away from me," she shouted.

Pacing, she told herself, "That did not happen. This is a dream. No, this is a nightmare. This is a nightmare." She pinched herself to see if she'd wake up. "No, God! Why? Why me?" she cried.

"Keisha, come on. We have to go before the cops

come," Andre pleaded, walking towards her.

Keisha turned to him and held up a hand to stop him. "Don't come near me! You are a cold-blooded murderer, just like your father," she said, breathing hard. Tears of fear pooled in her eyes.

Andre's face-hardened and his jaw twitched. "I'm nothin' like that piece of shit," he said between clenched teeth. He marched over to Keisha and looked her straight in the eyes. "I take care of my responsibilities and earned every fucking thing I got. I didn't steal it or take it, I *earned* it. Don't you ever forget that and don't you ever compare me to my father. Now get in the fuckin' car and let's go." He turned and stalked back to the car.

Keisha knew she'd pressed a sensitive button. Not wanting to take a chance on being his next victim, she walked over to the car and got in the back seat.

Andre had taken a towel from the trunk and was cleaning the mess she'd made on the front seat. He sighed. "Cuz, I'm sorry that you had to be a part of that. I've been looking for dude for a while now and was never able to catch him, so I had no choice."

"I don't care," she said, crying. "I don't want to be a part of this. Please, just drop me off."

Finished cleaning, he looked at Keisha and saw the fear in her eyes. "Okay, I'll drop you off, but let me explain myself." Walking around the car, he got in the driver's seat and started the car. Pulling off, he said, "I'm not gonna lie to you, this is what I do."

"What?" Keisha asked, her voice shaking. "Kill people?"

"Yes," Andre said.

"I thought you were a drug dealer, not an assassin,"

she said in disbelief.

"I never touched drugs a day in my life. That's what killed my mother. Don't you know how my mother died?"

"No."

"Well, let me tell you. I came home from school on a Friday afternoon and found her on the floor, shaking with foam coming out her mouth. I got a towel, wiped her mouth, and kissed her forehead. That's what she did to me to make me feel better. I was ten years old and didn't know no better. I didn't know what else to do. I couldn't dial 911 because it wasn't no phone in the house. My father didn't allow it because he said that was how the FBI tracks you. I remember seeing a needle and some white powder on the table next to where she was layin'. We was out in the boondocks and it wasn't no neighbors in walking distance, so I just sat there screaming for help and praying to God to wake my mother up. I held her for what seemed like forever." His voice trailed off.

Through the mirror, Keisha could see his eyes were red and he was fighting back tears.

"Ray, my coward-ass daddy, finally decided to come home after partying all weekend, doing God knows what." He sniffed, squeezing the steering wheel like it was his father's neck. He drove slowly, trying to maintain his composure. "He came in and found my momma and me on the floor. Her dead and me sitting in my own urine. For two days, I sat there in my own piss, scared to leave my momma's side. J.R. was at our grandparents' house. My mom took him over there Friday morning because he wasn't feeling good and she had some stuff to do. I made a promise to myself and swore on her grave that I'd never touch or go near drugs. That shit killed her.

The only woman I ever truly loved."

Keisha sat quietly. She had mixed emotions and didn't know what to think about Andre. He'd just shot some- one—taken a life—and then sat there and got emotional and teary-eyed while talking about his mother's death.

"I'm sort of a bounty hunter, cuz. The balance the dealers owe suppliers goes on their heads. I get rid of them and collect the fee."

"This is too much for me to take in right now," she said.

"Look, I'm up front with you about shit 'cause we family and I trust you. This shit out here is real. You can't owe people money and walk around like it ain't shit. Muthafuckas got pride and a rep to maintain. They have to make you an example. You will pay the price one-way or the other. If somebody fuck over you, what are you going to do when you get the opportunity to get their ass back? Let them slide and pray that they don't do it again or are you going to teach 'em a lesson?" He waited for an answer, but Keisha remained silent.

"You have to teach people how to treat you. And when you get the chance to get a muthafucka back who wronged you or the people you love, do it. This here will send out a clear message," he said, holding his pistol up. "You can't be naive. This is not *The Cosby Show* or *Good Times* where shit get worked out in thirty minutes. This shit here is real."

They pulled up in front of the hotel and the valet opened Keisha's door. "I understand if you never want to talk to me or kick it with me again," Andre said.

Keisha got out of the car without answering. She didn't know what to say or think or if she would ever kick it with him again. Her head was pounding and her stomach was growling. The last two days had been too much for her to handle.

Back in her room, she took two painkillers and washed them down with a Sprite. She walked into the bedroom, crawled into bed, and cried herself to sleep.

Chapter 5

"Sherrie, one day soon, this block will be a blur to me," Tameka said. The two of them sat on the steps of an abandoned building, tossing rocks onto the sidewalk. "I'm gonna save enough money to get the hell out of here."

Sherrie leaned back, propping on her elbows, and sighed. "Yeah, I want to get out of here too," she said. "And never come back."

Tameka continued, "I'm going to a neighborhood with manicured grass and recreational activities for kids. There won't be broken bottles all over the place, nobody outside arguing, fighting or doing drive-by shooting, and no rival blocks. Like Keisha's neighborhood seems to be. Sherrie, her neighborhood is so beautiful I felt like I was in another state. Her house is *amazing*."

"When did you go to her house?" Sherrie asked.

"The other day. Speaking of Keisha, have you spoken to her?" A car whizzed by playing loud music and she couldn't hear the response. "What you say?"

"No, have you?" Sherrie repeated.

"No. I haven't seen or heard from her since Friday

when she sent me a text saying she's staying at the Ritz-Carlton at the Water Tower Place."

"I thought she was staying at your house."

"Dino told her to get a room."

"I hate that bastard."

"Me too, girl. I hope they put his ass up *under* the jail. Let me call her right now." Taking out her phone, she dialed Keisha's number. When there was no answer, she sent a text.

"Man, it's slow out here today," Sherrie said.

"Yeah and it's Memorial Day weekend too. That's more of a reason why it supposed to be busy out here. It's a holiday."

A beat up black car with two guys in it pulled up.

The passenger leaned his head out the window. "Let me get three, Me-Me," he called to Tameka. Me-Me was her street name.

"Here, Tameka. Put one of mine with yours so that I can at least have ten dollars in my pocket," Sherrie said.

"A'ight, give it to me." Tameka turned and walked toward the car. "Come on, man, you know the routine. Get out the car," she instructed.

"Come on, Me-Me. You know me," he said rubbing his hands together.

"Yeah, I do. And you know the rules."

"Damn, you know you be giving a brotha a hard time," he said, getting out of the car. "I'm out, are you happy now? I need a favor, Me-Me. Let me hold one. You know I'm good for it. I'll bring you back fifteen bones later tonight."

"No, you know I don't operate like that. I need my

money now, not later. C.O.D."

"Come on, Me-Me. How long I been coppin' from you?"

"It don't matter."

"Over a year and I'm still not good for credit? That's fucked up. On the real, I don't shop with nobody but you. When you ain't out here, I call you. That's loyalty. Most people don't have that," he said, fidgeting and stepping from side to side.

Tameka didn't want to hear it. "Look, I don't do credit to protect both of us. I don't wanna have to kick your ass about my money. It eliminates the bullshit."

Sherrie, tired of hearing the crackhead plead his case, said, "Here you go. Just bring me my dub back tonight."

"Dub? I said fifteen."

"If you want credit, you gotta give me a dub."

He snatched the bag out Sherrie's hand and gave Tameka a funky look. "This some foul shit. You are definitely in the right business. You're a cold-hearted person, Me-Me." He shot another dirty look at her before climbing back into the car.

"Whatever. You got what you want, now get the fuck on." Tameka looked at Sherrie angrily. If looks could kill, Sherrie would've been a goner. "Sherrie, what the fuck was that?"

"What?"

"You trying to steal my customers?"

"No, I'm trying to help you keep your customers," Sherrie said, insulted.

"How? By giving him credit when I won't?"

"Exactly. You can't treat people like that and expect

them to come back."

"Oh, so now you got all the answers on making money in the streets," Tameka said sarcastically.

"No, but what I do know is that everybody wants a deal now and then. Dude has been copping from you for over a year. Why couldn't you give him credit?"

"Sherrie, listen, if you give one of them muthafuckas credit, all of 'em will be asking for it. You think they don't talk to each other? He comes to me because I have the best shit out here, not because of loyalty. That's the same dude that tried to sell me his dying mother's wedding ring. This is the street, not church. Out here, muthafuckas respect you more the worse you treat them. Treating them with kindness makes you look weak in their eyes. Don't be naive all your damn life, especially when it comes to these streets."

Sherrie knew Tameka was probably right and that she wasn't cut out for the street life. Just as she opened her mouth to speak, Tameka's phone rang.

"This better be Keisha's ass," Tameka said. Looking at the caller ID, her face lit up.

"Sherrie, this is that dude, June, from the park on the West Side."

"You mean his name isn't Romeo?" Sherrie said, rolling her eyes.

Tameka flipped her the middle finger and walked toward the vacant lot next to the building they were in front of.

"Hello," she answered softly.

June's smooth voice came through the line. "Hello, sweetie. How are you?"

She smiled. "I'm fine, and you?"

"Baby, I'm good now that I hear your voice. So what's on your agenda today?" he asked.

"Nothing much. Why? You have something planned for us to do?"

"As a matter of fact, I do."

"What?" Tameka asked, trying not to sound excited.

"It's a surprise. What's your address? I'll pick you up at eight."

"Are you familiar with the Southside? Do you feel comfortable coming out here?"

"Yes I am, and yes I do. I'm not the type of guy that only hang in one zip code, baby." He chuckled.

"You know how the Westside and Southside people feel about each other."

"No. What I know is how I feel about you, and I can't wait to see you. You've been on my mind heavy. Be dressed at eight sharp."

Tameka blushed like a teenager being asked out on her first date. "Okay, I'll be waiting." she said before ending the call. She rushed back to where Sherrie waited. "Come on," she said.

"Where are we going?" Sherrie asked.

"I have to go buy me a fit. I got a date," Tameka replied with a grin.

"A date with who? Romeo?"

"Yeah!"

"I'm going too. It's something about him that makes me feel uncomfortable."

"No you're not and it's something about him that makes me feel *very* comfortable."

"You ho," Sherrie muttered.

"If he play his cards right, I'll be his freaky little ho," Tameka said, then laughed at the look on Sherrie's face.

"Please don't tell me you're planning on sleeping with him tonight. On the first date? That's just nasty."

"Girl, listen to you. Sleeping with him period is nasty to you. I haven't had sex in six months. My girl is in desperate need of a tune-up," Tameka gyrated and winked at Tameka.

"I'll pray for you. Mother Mary, please forgive her, she doesn't know her vagina from a taxicab. Everybody who wave her down can get a ride." Sherrie laughed.

"Whatever, Sherrie. Like a cab, this ride costs."

Chapter 6

*K*eisha opened her eyes and stared at the ceiling. *Where the hell am I?* She looked around the dark room, confused, then realized she was at the hotel. She got out of bed and stumbled over her shoes on the way to the window. Opening the curtain, she shielded her eyes from the blinding sunlight.

Damn, I feel weak. What time it is? she asked herself. She picked up her cell phone and looked at the date and time. "Tuesday, 11:22. Oh, shit! I slept three days away. I shouldn't have kept taking those pills."

She saw that she had fifty-three missed calls. Scrolling through, she saw that Dino, Sherrie, Tameka, Dino's lawyer, and Andre had all called. Seeing her cousin's name brought back the memory of the murder she'd witnessed.

Shaking her head to clear her mind, she sat down to collect her thoughts and focus. She called Dino's lawyer first. On the third ring, a woman answered the phone.

"Barnes Law Office, how may we be of service to you," the perky voice said.

"Hello, Mr. Barnes please? This is Keisha Lee."

"Yes, Miss Lee, hold please, I'll see if he's available."

After a few seconds, the attorney's voice boomed through the phone. "Good morning, Miss Lee. I tried calling you yesterday. I'm at the courthouse. I've pulled Dino's file and we can have him home tonight. We'll discuss the cost later; I know he's good for it. Meet me here at two o'clock. It'll look good for him in the judge's eyes to see a family member present."

"Okay. I'll be there," Keisha said.

After hanging up, she went to the bathroom and turned on the shower. She wished she had time for a nice warm bath, but time wasn't on her side. She only had an hour and a half before she had to leave for the courthouse.

As soon as she dropped her robe to step into the shower, her cell phone rang. Picking it up from the counter, she saw it was an unknown number.

"Hello?" she said.

"Where the fuck you been? This is how you do me? I've been calling your fucking phone like crazy for the past few days. Bitch, you better not be out trickin' and spending my money."

Keisha was shocked speechless. Instead of being worried about her, his only concern was his money. He had no idea what she'd been through.

"Are you there?" he bellowed.

"Yes, I'm here." she said. She leaned against the counter with her arms crossed, cradling the phone between her ear and her shoulder.

"When I get out, I'm gonna kick yo' ass. Who the fuck were you with?"

At that moment, what Andre said came rushing back to her. *"You have to teach people how to treat you. And when you get the chance to get a muthafucka back who wronged you or the people you love, do it."*

"You better answer my question," Dino growled.

"You mean questions. Plural. First of all, I've been sleep for three fucking days from taking Tylenol with codeine. Second, you're not going to kick shit. Last, but not least, I don't have to spend your money. If I had been out tricking, I would've gotten paid. Remember, you made me a hot brand. A hot commodity," she mocked.

"Oh, so you got balls now, huh? A nigga behind bars, so you think you can say what the fuck you want to me and get away with it?"

"No, you ignorant bastard. Women can't grow those. What I did grow is self-respect. I'll see your sorry ass in court."

Keisha turned the phone off, went into the bedroom, and tossed it on the bed. She'd never spoken to Dino like that before and it felt good. She was proud of herself, but she knew she'd pay for it later if he got out. She dialed room service and ordered. When it arrived, she ate and then took her shower.

Under the showerhead, letting the warm water run down her face and body, she felt as though it was cleansing her from all the pain and regret she had for not standing up to Dino a long time ago. She congratulated herself for regaining her voice and her strength.

"Ms. Lee, the charges against Dino will not hold up I court," Dick Barnes, Dino's lawyer, told Keisha in the hallway outside the courtroom. "They did not have a search warrant or permission to enter the property. I can get them dismissed immediately, however, the parole officer will be in contact with him once he gets wind of this."

"Mr. Barnes, is there somewhere we can talk privately?"

"Sure," he said.

Keisha and the attorney stepped into a non-descript office. After speaking with him briefly, she walked into the courtroom and patiently waited for Dino's name to be called.

"The court calls Dino Alexander Hill."

A chill of fear surged through Keisha's body when the officer escorted Dino out. Wearing his jail uniform, a dingy blue shirt and pants, he looked confident of gaining his freedom. When he spotted Keisha, he winked at her.

He must really think I'm stupid or his ass is bipolar, she thought. She played along by winking back and giving a little wave.

Mr. Barnes stepped to the podium. "Your Honor, I will be speaking on the behalf of Mr. Hill."

"And you are?" the judge asked.

"Your Honor, I am Dick Barnes, Mr. Hill's attorney."

"Okay. Mr. Hill, you are being charged with possession of an illegal substance. Your records reflect a history of the same charges and that you are currently on parole. How do you plead?"

"Mr. Hill pleads guilty, Your Honor."

"What?" Dino said, looking at his lawyer, his eyes wide.

"Trust me, Dino, I know what I'm doing," the attorney whispered, patting him on the back.

"Mr. Hill, is there a problem? Do you not wish to

plead guilty?" the judge asked, an eyebrow raised.

"Trust me, Dino. Have I ever let you down?" Mr. Hill asked.

Confused, Dino turned to look at the judge. "No, your Honor. There's no problem. I plead guilty like my attorney stated."

"Okay, Mr. Hill, you are hereby sentenced to five years for violation of your parole and another four years for possession of an uncontrolled substance. I really hope that you learn your lesson this time around."

Dino's eyes turned blood red. Looking at his lawyer, he yelled, "What the fuck did you do?"

"Dino, calm down. I'll straighten this out. I promise you'll be out in no time."

"I'm gonna kill you," Dino shouted. He head-butted the attorney, knocking him to the floor, and proceeded to stomp on him. Two court officers rushed over and tackled Dino, forcing him down. One placed his knee in the center of Dino's back and pinned his head to the floor.

Keisha moved to where Dino could see her. She smoothed the fabric of her skintight, leopard print dress and blew him a kiss. Winking, she gave him a little finger wave before strutting out of the courtroom like a supermodel, her sling-back heels clicking every step.

Dino's eyes filled with tears of fury as he started putting the pieces together. *How could she do this to me? After all I did for her. That bitch will be dead by midnight,* he thought as the guards picked him up and escorted him out.

Keisha stood outside of the courthouse, soaking in the sunlight. Spotting her when he came out, the attorney lowered the makeshift icepack he'd been holding to his head and walked over to her. She handed him a thick envelope with a rubber band around it.

"Here's the other half. I told you I'm a woman of my word. That's more than you would have made off him in ten years. And, don't forget, I want my mother committed to a rehab facility."

"No problem. Nice doing business with you, Ms. Lee." Looking her up and down, he smiled. "Would you like to join me for a late lunch?"

"Sorry, my days of laying down with snakes are over. The bites are too hard to treat and often deadly." Turning, she put on her shades and walked toward her car.

Finally, she was at peace. She wasn't worried about the consequences of the streets. She wasn't worried about anything or anybody. For the first time in her life, she felt totally free.

Today looks like a nice day to go shopping. Putting her purse on the passenger seat, she hooked her iPod into the car's radio and drove off to Beyonce's, *Me, myself and I.*

Chapter 7

*A*fter her shopping spree, Keisha returned to the hotel to gather her belongings and check out. She knew Dino would make a call to the hood and have his goons get at her by the next day. She had to make her next move quickly.

Looking for a hotel on the north side of town, where she knew no one would look for her, she came across an open house sign for a two-bedroom condo in a beautiful, red brick building directly across from Lincoln Park Zoo.

Keisha walked into the rental unit and immediately fell in love with the spacious, open kitchen equipped with stainless steel appliances and stained maple cabinets. She paced the kitchen slowly, admiring the black granite countertops with glass backsplash tiles and recessed lighting reflecting off the hardwood bamboo floors. *I'm not much of a cook, but this look like it will be my favorite spot in the house for sure,* she thought.

Moving to the living room, she saw an exposed brick wall with a radiant gas fireplace. Double glass doors led to a balcony overlooking Lincoln Park. From the center of the balcony, a telescope gave an amazing view of Lake Michigan and the city.

In the master bedroom, she found a huge walk-in closet, a granite vanity area with his and hers motion sinks, separate showers, and a garden tub. It was a personal oasis with all the luxury of an upscale spa.

Returning to the living room, she continued to look around.

I have to get this.

"May I help you?" An Asian woman appeared out of nowhere, holding a worn brown briefcase.

Keisha turned. Given the lady's navy blue pencil skirt, blazer, and name tag, she figured this must be the realtor. "Yes, you may. How much are you leasing this unit for?"

The sales agent looked Keisha up and down before answering, as if trying to figure her out.

"It leases for eighteen hundred a month. Your income has to be three times the amount of the rent and you must have good credit."

Keisha smiled and returned to admiring the wall décor. "Did you say eighteen hundred?"

"Yes."

"Do you have the lease agreement with you?"

The realtor look irritated as she exhale. "It doesn't work like that. You have to fill out an application and pay the twenty-five dollar administrative fee upfront and then we process your information. It could take three to five days. And there are applicants ahead of you."

Keisha opened up her Dior bag and pulled out two stacks of hundred dollar bills and one stack on fifties. Holding them up, she tossed them to the realtor. The lady dropped her briefcase to catch them.

"This should cover a year up front and something left

over for you to treat yourself to something nice."

The woman's eyes widened, then she grinned. Keisha knew she'd never received that much money upfront before.

"Yes, Mrs.—"

"No, it's *Miss*. Miss Keisha Lee." Keisha said, looking through the balcony door at her view of the park.

After they finished the paperwork and Keisha got the keys to her new place, she went shopping for a bed and other household items.

Keisha set a bouquet of roses on the counter to add life to her new place. Dino didn't like flowers in the house, saying they reminded him of death. Keisha bent down to smell them and thought of Sherman. He was the first guy to ever buy her flowers. Dino had bought her expensive gifts, but never flowers.

She decided to give her former classmate a call to see how he was doing. After running down to her car to get the card he'd given her with his cell number on it, she called him. The phone rang three times and just as she was about to hang up, a male voice answered.

"Hello, may I speak to Sherman?" she said.

"This is Sherman speaking."

"Hey, you, how have you been? This is Keisha."

"Well, hello, Miss Lady. I must admit, I didn't think you would call."

"Well, why'd you give me your number?" she said, laughing.

"Wishful thinking. I couldn't let you go without trying one last time."

Keisha rolled her eyes and smiled, twirling her hair with a finger. He'd been persistent in trying to hook up with her throughout their whole four years of school.

"Whatever. So, what you been up to?"

"Nothing much. Just working, trying to stay above water."

"Same here. What's on your agenda for tonight? "

"Nothing," he responded quickly.

"Would you like to come hang out with me?" she asked, knowing what his answer would be.

"Uh, sure," he answered, sounding shocked by her invitation. "I'd like that very much."

"What time are you available?"

"Now," he said without hesitation.

Keisha giggled. She could hear the excitement in his voice. "Come on over so we can hang. I'll order us a spinach deep-dish pizza from Giordano's. I remember you said that's your favorite."

"Yes, it is."

Keisha gave him the address and told him to call when he was downstairs.

While waiting for the pizza and Sherman to arrive, she took a shower to freshen up. Afterward, she lotioned up and applied shimmering powder to her breasts, then sprayed a lightly-scented fragrance behind her ears and between her thighs. Just as she stepped into a silk backless dress, her phone rang. It was Sherman. *Damn that was fast. He beat the pizza guy,* she thought.

"Hello."

"Hey Keisha, I'm at the store. Would you like me to bring you something?"

"Yes, can you bring a radio?"

"A what?" he asked, confused.

"A boom box. I don't have one and we'll need some music to listen to. The docking station for my iPod is broken. I'll give you the money for it when you get here."

"The money's not a problem, sweetie. You just took me by surprise asking for a radio. Most people ask for soda or chips," he said, laughing.

"I thought you noticed that I'm not like most," she said seductively.

"No, you most definitely are not. I'll be there in a minute."

"Okay, see you when you get here."

A few minutes later, the pizza was delivered. After Keisha paid the delivery guy and he left, she realized she didn't have any plates. Her phone rang again. It was Sherman calling to say he was downstairs. She looked down over the balcony and saw him standing at the door with the boom box in one hand and a six pack of soda in the other, smiling. Going to the intercom by the front door, she buzzed him and instructed him to come to the top floor.

Out of breath when he reached her door, he asked "Why did you choose the top floor?"

"To save me time at the gym." She laughed and took the radio and soda out of his hands.

"Nice crib."

"Thanks, feel free to look around."

She walked to the kitchen and put the sodas in the

refrigerator, keeping two out for them to drink. Set up the radio on the counter, she turned on her favorite station.

"Did you just move in?"

"Yes, today actually. You are my first houseguest. Welcome to my castle," she said, making a sweeping motion with her hands.

"I feel honored. Your place is really nice, empty and all." He walked onto the balcony and looked through the telescope. "This is an awesome view. Is this the real reason you chose the top floor?"

"Exactly the reason. I love the view," Keisha said, bringing the pizza over to a blanket she'd laid on the floor before he arrived. "I hope you're hungry, I order us a large pizza. I apologize, but I don't have any plates or utensils, so we have to eat out of the box and use our hands."

"Is there any other way to eat pizza?" Sherman asked, coming to sit with her.

"So, where are you working?

"The same place. I got promoted after we graduated."

"That fast?"

"Yes, today I started my new position. I've been with the company since I was sixteen. I started in the mailroom. Now, I'm working in the marketing department."

Keisha smiled. "Next, you'll have the corner office."

"That's the plan," he said. "What about you?" he asked, grabbing a slice of pizza and taking a huge bite.

"I've never worked before. I don't think a company would hire me at the pay I want with no experience."

"Not to be nosy, but how can you afford this place if you don't work?"

"My father takes care of it."

Sherman was cool, but Keisha wasn't about to tell him her life story. She just wanted to chill with someone who didn't know about her troubled past and wouldn't judge her. Her phone rang and she turned it off.

"You don't have to do that for me," he said, pointing to her cell phone.

"I did that for me, not you. I want to enjoy our time together without any interruptions."

Keisha got up and turned the volume on the radio up. Old school hip-hop blared through the speakers.

"This song used to be the *business*," Keisha said. She started rapping with the song. "I met this girl when I was ten years old. And what I loved most she had so much soul."

"What you know about Common Sense?" Sherman asked, teasing. "My mistake, he dropped the 'Sense.' What do you know about Common? You were too young to know about this song."

"My best friend's cousin used to play hip-hop all day and all night. I can beatbox too."

"Get out of here." He laughed.

Keisha pursed her lips and started beatboxing, showing her skills. Sherman joined in, rapping and beatboxing along with her.

"That was tight," she said when they stopped. "You got some skills, boy. Why didn't you pursue a career in entertainment?"

"I need something steady. Plus, my parents weren't having that. And besides that, I got a child to feed."

Keisha's eyes widened. "You have a child? I didn't

know that. You never mention her."

"Yep. Here's a picture of her. On that picture she was three, she's five now."

"She's cute. Must look like her mother. No, I'm kidding!" she said, laughing at the expression on his face. "She looks just like you. What's her name?"

"Patrice Shavonta Johnson. She's my heart. Daddy's little girl who can do no wrong, at least in my eyes she can't. She's the reason I stay focused and do what I have to. It's easy to get distracted out here."

"I know what you're saying. Are your parents still together?"

"Yeah, thirty years strong. What about yours?"

"They're divorced. Well, not divorced, but separated." She shrugged.

Sherman could tell by the look on her face and her tone that she didn't want to discuss her parents, so he changed the subject. "Do you know which star is which?" he asked, going over to the telescope.

"No," she admitted.

"Come here, let me show you."

Keisha looked through the eyepiece and he got behind her, guiding the telescope and pointing at the stars. "First," he said, "let me tell you about the brightest star in the sky, Sirius, also known as the Dog Star, Its name comes from the Greek word for scorching."

Sherman continued to talk, pointing out stars and telling her about them, but Keisha stopped listening. The smell of his cologne and the feel of his hard chest pressed against her back distracted her and all she could think of was having him inside her. She used to daydream about him often in class, but thought it would never happen.

His breath softly blowing against her ear while he spoke sent her over the edge and she couldn't contain herself any longer. Touching his hand, she asked, "Are you cold?"

"No, I'm comfortable, It feels good in here. It's a beautiful night," he replied.

"Your hands feel cold. Let me warm them for you." Grabbing his hands, she placed them underneath her dress and between her thighs.

He gently kissed the back of her neck, taking in the smell of her sweet fragrance as he caressed her, rubbing his hands up and down her thighs, pulling her close to him. He slid a hand into her panties and positioned a fingertip on her clit. Keisha moaned and moved against his hand as his finger gently rubbed up and down. He moved his finger deep into her core and continued massaging her pearl with his thumb. Keisha's head fell back on his shoulder and she sighed in pleasure before nipping on his earlobe. Removing his hand, he turned her around and kissed her, his tongue darting between her lips.

Keisha unfastened his pants, allowing them to fall to the floor, before stepping back and removing her thong. Sliding her dress straps off her shoulders, the silky fabric pooled at her feet, leaving her naked form silhouetted in the moonlight.

Sherman couldn't believe this was happening. He'd lusted for Keisha since the first day he'd seen her and had grown to like and respect her the more he'd gotten to know her. He picked her up and carried her to the bedroom. Laying her down on her stomach, he lightly squeezed her buttocks, kissing each cheek. Silently thanking God, he knelt between her legs and parted her inner lips with his tongue, licking, sucking and massaging her.

Keisha screamed, moaned, and bit her pillow. "I want to feel you in me, baby" she said.

After grabbing a condom from his pants pocket and slipping it on, he flipped her over. Bending over her, he kissed her on the lips, then moved to suck on a nipple before sitting back up and sliding into her. Her warmth fit him like a glove. Lifting one of her legs over his shoulder, he began to move, slowly at first, then lowered her leg and increased his pace.

Meeting him thrust for thrust, Keisha had never experienced the sensations his movements caused. A pressure built, so she told him to stop, she had to pee.

"Baby, no you don't," he moaned. "Just keep rolling those hips."

Still matching his movements, she said, "Yes, I do, please stop."

"Trust me, baby, you don't have to pee. Just let it happen."

Keisha wanted him get up, but he felt so good sliding in and out of her that she couldn't bring herself to stop him. *If he wants me to piss on him, I will,* she thought, closing her eyes and giving in to the pleasure.

Then she exploded. She cried out as her body spasmed, her toes curling and her eyes watering. Her vaginal walls pulsated, squeezing Sherman's hardness in her. She dug her fingers into his back as he moved faster, pulling her hair gently and sucking on her neck. Kissing her, he stilled and moaned into her mouth when his own climax erupted.

Afterward, he kissed her on the forehead before rolling to lie beside her. "Thanks for trusting me," he said, removing the condom and dropping it into the trashcan next to the bed.

"Uh huh, no problem. Thank you." Keisha said, still breathless and amazed.

"Can you get me a towel?" he asked.

"Sure." She tried to move, but she couldn't. Her legs were too weak. "Sherman, promise me that you won't laugh."

"Okay, I promise. What?"

"I can't move. My legs are stuck. You have to go get yourself a towel. They're in the linen closet in the hallway."

"No problem. Would you like me to bring you one? And maybe a bottle of water?" he asked with a smirk.

"Please do."

He got up and left the room chuckling.

Keisha took a deep breath and blew it out. *I thought Dino showed me everything*, she thought. *I can't let Sherman think he got one up on me. Even though he did. I can't go out like that.*

Sherman walked back into the room and handed her a bottle of water. "Here you go, baby," he said.

Keisha sat up and gulped half the water before setting the bottle on the nightstand and pulling her hair into a ponytail. Positioning him on the bed, she got on her knees between his legs and asked him for the time.

"It's one-fifty-three," he said, looking at her questioningly.

Winking at him, she leaned over and took all ten inches of him into her mouth. his eyes bulged as he watched her suck him, her jaws sinking in and her head bobbing up and down. He closed his eyes and laid his head back against the headboard, enjoying the feel of her mouth stroking him to erection again. Moaning, she moved her mouth up and down his shaft, making small circles on the tip of his dick with her tongue and massaging his balls with one hand. Feeling him stiffen, she sucked harder and faster. He tried to push her up, but she wouldn't let him. Wrapping her arms around his waist, she deep throated him, forcing him to cum in her mouth.

After his release, Sherman fell back on the bed and lay as if he were in a daze. Keisha grabbed the towel he'd gotten for her and wiped her mouth, spitting his cum into it. "What time is it?" she asked.

He looked at his watch. Smiling, he said, "It's one fifty-six." *Damn,* he thought. *She sucked me off in three minutes. Hell, I think that's faster than Super Head.*

"Now we're even," she said, standing up and moving to walk away.

Before she could step away, he pulled her back into bed, on top of him. Holding her in place, he looked at her and smiled. "So you like to compete, huh?"

"No," she said, kissing him. "I like to satisfy."

"Sweetie, I was satisfied with the phone call. But I am enjoying the treats that came along with the pizza."

"Me too, baby" Keisha said softly, playing with the silky, baby-fine hair on his chest. "Now, let's go for round two," she said, kissing him again.

Chapter 8

*A*fter Sherman left the next morning, Keisha turned her cell phone on and saw that she had several voice messages. She turned on the speakerphone and listened to the calls while she brushed her teeth.

Tameka's voice boomed on the first two. "Keisha, where the hell are you? Sherrie and I been calling you. We went to the hotel you were supposed to be staying at and they said you checked out. Call me as soon as you get this message."

"Keisha, we're starting to worry. Where in the fuck are you and why aren't you answering your phone?"

"Hello, sister, this is Sherrie, I hope everything is okay with you. I pray for your safety and return. Keisha, know that our Father doesn't give us more then we can handle. I love you."

"Hey, Lady Bug, this is Sincere. Call me when you get this message. I have something important to tell you. Make sure you call me back ASAP. Peace and love, my sweetie."

"Keisha, you ain't got to be scared of that Negro. We

got yo' back. You don't have to hide," Tameka said.

What is she talking about? Keisha's other line beeped. She looked at the caller ID and saw that it was Sincere.

After rinsing her mouth, she answered. "Hello?"

"Hey, Keisha, this is Sincere."

"I know. What's up, lady?"

"I was just about to ask you the same thing. Sweetie, I have to tell you something. Are you by yourself?"

"Yeah," Keisha said slowly, wondering what was going on and starting to worry.

"Okay, what I'm about to tell you, you can't let *anyone* know that I told you."

"I won't, girl, you know me. What is it?"

Sincere took a deep breath and exhaled. "Dino put a hit out on you. He's offering ten G's."

Keisha gasped. She'd known Dino would seek revenge, but she never thought he'd want her dead.

"Are you there?" Sincere asked.

"Yes, I'm here." Keisha's voice shook.

"He said you paid his lawyer to throw his case."

"Why would he think I'd do something like that?"

Sincere knew that to get out of a controlling and abusive relationship, a woman will do whatever it takes to escape. It was clear to her that Keisha had gotten a chance and took it.

"Listen, Keisha, I've been where you are. I know firsthand there's no limit to what a woman will do to get out of a life-threating situation. Baby, just be careful."

"I will. Do you know who he put on me?"

"Yeah, it's the Jones boys. You know those grimy-ass,

broke bums don't value their own lives or anybody else's."

"Are they the only ones?"

"As far as I know. I don't think he trusts anyone but them to get the job done."

"Sincere, thank you. I won't breathe a word of this to anyone. And don't worry. I'll be all right."

"Okay, sweetie. I love you. Be careful."

"I love you too and I will. Peace and love."

"Peace and love, Keisha."

As soon as Keisha hung up, the phone rang again. It was Tameka.

"What's up?" Keisha said.

"'What's up?' All you got to fucking say is 'What's up?' Bitch, where in the hell have you been? We've been all over Chicago, worried sick, looking for your ass!" Tameka yelled.

"I've been taking care of my business. I needed some air. Sorry I didn't call y'all."

"Sherrie, come get this phone. This inconsiderate bitch..."

Sherrie's voice came on the line. "Hey, sis, I'm glad you're all right. We've been worried out of our minds about you. Don't ever do that again! When you hurt, we hurt, Keisha. We're here for you."

"I know y'all are. Why were you guys so worried?"

"We know Dino went to court and probably got out. We didn't know if he kidnapped you or what."

"Oh, Dino didn't get out," Keisha announced.

"Word?" Sherrie said, surprised.

"Yeah, he actually got sentenced to nine years."

Sherrie couldn't contain her excitement. "Tameka, come here," she screamed. "Dino got nine years."

"Get the fuck outta here," Tameka said. She snatched the phone from Sherrie. "Why did he get nine years, Keisha?"

"I'll tell you everything in person. Dino isn't our worry anymore, the Jones boys are."

Tameka frowned. "What?"

"Yeah, meet me at my condo."

"Condo?" Tameka was still confused.

"Yeah, I told you I was taking care of some business."

After giving Tameka the address, Keisha got in the tub. Soaking in a bubble bath, she tried to come up with a plan. She knew that the Jones boys would try their very best to kill her for the reward. Assuming that Dino didn't have any money to pay them because she had it all, she thought about paying them herself. She discarded that idea, knowing they'd think that she was soft and would try to extort money from her every chance they got, especially with her not having a man in the streets to protect her.

Sighing, she sank deeper into the bubbles. *I'll think of something. Until then, I'm not going to stress myself about it.* She lay back and thought about her night with Sherman. He'd shown her positions she'd never known existed and she'd lost count of how many times she'd cum.

"Damn, that man got skills," she said, rubbing her thigh.

An hour later, Keisha opened the door to let her friends in. She had gone through and discarded anything that even suggested she'd had company. She knew

Tameka and Sherrie would go through the house with a fine-tooth comb.

"Damn, girl. You snapped the hell out," Tameka said, looking out at the balcony.

"This place looks nice empty. I can imagine how it'll look with furniture," Sherrie said, rubbing a hand over the granite kitchen counter.

"Thank you." Keisha was pleased with the compliments about her new place.

"When'd you get this?" Tameka asked.

"Yesterday," Keisha said.

"Where's my room?" Sherrie asked, joking.

"Let's go get something to eat. I have something very important to tell y'all," Keisha said.

"Please, don't tell me you're pregnant," Tameka said.

"Hell no, I'm not pregnant. I wouldn't have a baby by that douche bag. I took extra precautions remember"

At eighteen, Keisha had found herself three months pregnant with Dino's baby. Around that time was when their relationship took a turn for the worst. She had refused to have a baby by him and be trapped for the rest of her life. Without telling him about the pregnancy, she'd had an abortion and gotten her tubes tied, She'd allowed him to think that he was shooting blanks and couldn't get her pregnant, knowing he wasn't the type of guy who would go to the doctor and get check out.

"Oh yeah, that's right," Tameka said, following Keisha out the door.

"That doctor knew you weren't thirty-five years old," Sherrie said, recalling the trip to the doctor's office. "His trifling behind just wanted your money. Good thing you can get them untied."

"One thing Dino taught me was that money can get you anything."

Tameka nodded. "That's true."

A few minutes later, they pulled up at Golden Nuggets, just down the street from Keisha's house. She knew it wasn't safe for her to go to the hood or anywhere near the Southside yet. They ordered their meals and Keisha filled them in on what happened in court and what Sincere had told her. Tameka and Sherrie stood with their mouths open, shocked. Mostly because they didn't believe Keisha had the balls to pull something like that on Dino, but also because they were scared for her.

"So what are you gonna do?" Sherrie asked with tears in her eyes. She knew the Jones boys were nothing to play with. Rumor had it that they'd killed their own father for cheating on and beating their mom. They'd grown tired of watching him abuse her, so they'd hung him in the basement and made it look like he committed suicide.

Tameka folded her arms across her chest. "What do you mean, what is she going to do? We're gonna kill those bastards before they get her."

"I've never taken a life before. It's not as easy as you might think, Tameka. And you'll pay the price of eternal life in hell," Sherrie said.

"So, would you rather lose Keisha now or suffer the consequence in the afterlife? Plus, isn't this hell right here? Shit, life is a living hell," Tameka retorted.

Sherrie was torn. She had been raised Catholic and, although she regularly committed the sin of selling an illegal substance, she'd tricked herself into believing that she was helping others by putting the majority of the money into the offering plate at the church. She knew that murder was right up there with taking your own life, it was the ultimate sin. But, for the love of her sister, she was willing sacrifice her eternal life.

"No, Tameka, I'm just saying. There has to be something else we can do."

"Ladies, don't worry about it. I'm not scared or concerned. The Jones boys picked the right chick to fuck with this time. No more fucking or getting over on Keisha. No. From this day forward *I'm* doing all the fucking." Keisha wore a determined look on her face as she sipped her drink.

"What are you going to do?" Tameka asked.

"Didn't you tell me the other day that the two gangs over there are at war?" Keisha asked.

"Yeah," Tameka said, shrugging.

"And the eldest Jones is the leader, right?"

"Yeah. Why?" Tameka was confused.

Keisha didn't respond. She was busy figuring out her strategy. She wasn't gonna pay anybody so that she could stay alive. She'd rather someone kill the person who planned to kill her.

It suddenly clicked to Tameka and Sherrie exactly what Keisha was planning. They didn't even need to discuss the details. They exchanged knowing glances and smiled.

"After breakfast, I'm taking y'all shopping," Keisha said. "Plus, I need to get some furniture. Not a word, Tameka. Miss Independent, let me do this, okay?"

"No problem," Tameka said.

"You know I don't have a problem," Sherrie said.

"Then it's settled. Woodfield Mall, here we come!"

Chapter 9

"*W*hat's up, cuz? I thought I'd never hear from you again. Glad you decided to call," Andre said.

"Cuz, I'm in some hot shit," Keisha confessed.

"What's going on?" He sat up. She had his full attention now.

"Can you come to my house so we can talk?"

"I'm on my way. What's the address?" Keisha gave him her address and hung up.

When he arrived, Keisha told him everything. He was proud of his cousin for taking the risk that she did, but upset that there was a bid on her head.

"Don't worry about nothin'," he said. "I got you. We'll work your plan and add something to it."

"What are we going to do?" she asked, relieved that she had some help.

"Find out where his main bitch live and that's where you get him. See, no man want everybody to know his main spot. Lay low for about a month or two. I'll hook you up with a guy to get you a piece. Keep it on you at all times."

Keisha offered to pay him, but he refused to take the money.

"We're family. This is what family do. We take care of each other. Don't worry, you ain't out here by yourself. I got you."

Keisha did everything her cousin told her to do. She laid low for a month, enjoying nights with Sherman and taking shooting lessons at a range in the suburbs. In the meantime, the beef between the two gangs grew. Every few days, Tameka and Sherrie came to visit and would tell her who had gotten shot or killed. After a while, though, Keisha got tired of hiding out. She was ready to execute her plan.

Late one night, as planned, she met up with Andre and got in the hooptie he used to do his dirty work. They drove straight to Reggie Jones' girlfriend's house. Reggie was the eldest of the brothers and Andre had done some research in the streets and found out he posted up regularly at his girl's place on Ingleside Street. They drove around the block a few times, making sure no one was out. Reggie's black Chevy Impala was parked in front of the house just as they had expected. Andre parked in the alley and Keisha got out. She crept over to Reggie's car and pushed it hard to make the alarm go off. Then she stooped down, hiding.

Hearing the alarm, Reggie looked out, but didn't see anyone near his car. He turned the alarm off and moved away from the window.

Keisha bumped the car three more times.

Finally, he got fed up and came outside to see what was going on.

By this time, Keisha was standing in the opening

between his house and the neighbor's. Reggie circled around his car with his pistol out, looking for damage to it or someone hiding behind it. He didn't see anything, so he started back toward the house. Putting his pistol back in his waistband, he heard a girl's voice call his name.

"What's up, Reggie?" Keisha said from her position.

"Who that?" he said, looking around.

"Who you been looking for?"

"I've been looking for a lot of people."

Keisha walked out into the light. Reggie saw her and froze.

"Where you been, girl?" he said, startled. Noticing her all black attire and leather gloves, he wondered what was up.

"Oh, I've been around," she said calmly.

"So, how's Dino holding up?" he asked.

"You tell me. Or should I ask your girl?"

"What?"

"You know Dino was fucking your bitch, right?" Keisha laughed. "Honestly, what girl wasn't he fucking around here? Did you think yours was off limits?" She put her hands on her hips. She knew no man wanted to imagine his girl getting fucked by someone else, especially a guy with more to offer financially than him. "Nigga you can't be that full of yourself that you think a bitch going to turn down fucking a nigga with money."

Reggie's jaw tightened. He was pissed, knowing there was possibly some truth to what she was saying. He started stuttering and pacing, obviously agitated. Stopping, he turned to face Keisha, a murderous gleam in his eyes, and reached for his pistol.

Andre eased up behind him and put his 9mm to Reggie's head. "I don't think that would be a wise thing to do, my man," he said.

Keisha moved closer and got face to face with Reggie. "Ten G's was all it took for you to kill me, huh? We grew up together. My pops fed and clothed your turncoat ass and your snot-nosed little brothers. He practically raised you and you were willing to take me out for a lousy ten stacks?"

"So, you gonna kill me, Keisha? Then do what the fuck you came to do. If not, you and this punk get the fuck out my face and off my block."

Andre hit Reggie in the back of the head with the pistol handle and knocked him to the ground.

Reggie tried to get up.

"Negro, shut your sloppy, fat ass the fuck up." Andre said. He kicked Reggie in the ass and he fell back to the ground. "Bitch-ass muthafucka. You didn't know who you was fuckin' with, huh? You thought she was out here by herself?" Do you not know who we are?"

"Nigga, fuck you and that bitch," Reggie said, trying to get up from the pavement.

Andre unloaded one in his leg and he fell back to the ground. Now scared, knowing Andre meant business, he scooted away. Grabbing his injured leg, he tried to reason his way out of the situation.

"Keisha, I was never going to harm you. We're like family. You know we cool. I wasn't paying Dino no attention. I was gonna take the money and that's it! I promise on my kids' life."

"Shut the hell up," Andre growled. "Keisha, shoot this bitch. This nigga pleading for his life and on his own land. This is really some hilarious shit." He chuckled and shook his head. "Man the fuck up and take this shit. Live by the gun, die by the gun!"

Keisha walked to Reggie and stood over him, pointing her gun at his head with her finger on the trigger. Unable to do it, she stood there.

Andre saw her hesitation. "Keisha, listen to me. This is the same muthafucka who was gonna kill you."

Swallowing, she pulled the trigger back lightly and released it. She couldn't bring herself to shoot him. She let her arm drop and turned away. Reggie exhaled loudly.

Andre turned his gun from Reggie to Keisha. "Turn your ass back around and killed this fat, stanky muthafucka or I'll kill you. And we both know I won't hesitate."

Reggie watched them, his eyes wide.

Keisha was scared. She knew Andre was crazy. Raising the gun, she closed her eyes and squeezed the trigger, emptying the weapon into Reggie's chest and stomach.

When she finished, Andre pointed his gun at Reggie's head and fired three bullets into his skull.

"Now, you can have your block back, bitch-ass nigga," Andre said, sneering at the lifeless body. He turned to look at Keisha. "You have to make sure the muthafucka is dead before you leave. Come on. Let's bounce."

They ran to the car, drove to the lake, and threw the guns in the water. Keisha felt relieved, but nervous and scared. She couldn't believe she had just killed somebody. Nor could she believe that Andre, her own cousin, had threatened to shoot her.

While setting their clothes on fire, she turned to him. "Were you really gonna shoot me?" she asked.

"Hell naw. I had to make you do what you needed

to do. You had to realize it was either him or you," he explained.

"It doesn't bother you?"

"What, the killing?"

"Yeah."

"No. And it shouldn't bother you either. It gets easier every time."

Keisha wondered how many lives Andre had taken, but she didn't ask. He drove her back to her car and they parted ways.

Back at her house, Keisha couldn't sleep. Nervous, she paced the floor. She worried that the police would come knocking at her door to arrest her at any second. Going to the kitchen, she poured herself a glass of wine to calm her nerves.

I did what I had to do. It was either him or me.

She leaned against the balcony doors, sipping her wine and staring at the stars in the dark sky.

After tonight, my life will never be the same. Innocent Keisha is dead and gone.

Though still scared of the repercussions of the law and the streets, she felt empowered and ready to take on the world.

The buzzing of the doorbell woke Keisha from a deep sleep.

"Who is it?" she asked through the intercom.

"It's us, Keisha. Buzz us up," Tameka said.

Before they were completely in the door, Tameka

announced, "Girl, Reggie's dead."

"What?" Keisha said in mock shock.

Tameka crossed her arms. "Girl, don't play that dumb shit with us. We know who did it."

"Who did it?"

"A'ight, you can play deaf, dumb, and retarded if you want to."

"Tameka, Keisha wouldn't do anything like that. Would you?" Sherrie asked, praying Keisha would say no.

Keisha ignored the question. She didn't want to lie to her girls. Instead of answering, she walked to the kitchen and took some food out of the fridge to cook.

"Y'all want some breakfast?"

"Yes, we do" Sherrie said, kicking her shoes off.

"Hey, Mrs. Butterworth, word is that Reggie was broke," Tameka said.

"What? I thought he had money," Keisha said.

"No. Everything he had was a front. His brothers are walking around looking stupid, talking about what they're gonna do. The man over Reggie called the war off. He said he was losing too much money over nonsense. He met up with the dude over the other gang and called a truce. So the Jones boys are pissed 'cause they can't retaliate without suffering the consequences."

"Damn, I thought Reggie was one of the big men," Keisha said, shocked at the news.

"Nope. Reggie was the soldier, the send-off guy. He wasn't smart enough to be a leader. He could only lead those stupid-ass brothers of his. People were only scared of them 'cause everybody knew they wouldn't hesitate to pull the trigger. On top of all that, the big man refused to give them money to bury Reggie. He said they started the war. He said they made him lose money and it's because of them their brother is dead, so they need to find a way to bury him."

"For real?" Keisha flipped over a pancake, digesting what she'd heard.

"Yep." Tameka said, walking over to look in the skillet. "Girl, who taught you how to make pancakes? These boys look just like the ones at IHOP. Now, are you ready for the good news?"

"I thought that *was* the good news," Keisha said.

"No, it gets better. I heard they asked Dino for the money and he told them he didn't have it."

"Get the hell outta here." Keisha said, dropping her spatula.

"Yep. So you don't have shit to worry about. How can he pay them to murk you if he can't pay 5G's for their brother's funeral?" Tameka reasoned.

"Keisha breathed easier. She could come and go as she pleased and she'd finally gotten revenge on Dino. She'd come out on top. She had all his money.

Tameka looked over at Sherrie on the sofa with her feet up. "Sherrie, why you so quiet?"

"I'm ignoring the whole conversation y'all having and enjoying my home-cooked meal."

"Girl, please. You eat a home-cooked meal every day. Your mother cooks for you," Keisha said.

"Keisha, we got to go," Tameka said. "Since its safe on the block again, I need to go make me some money."

"You don't have to hustle on the block anymore, I got

y'all," Keisha said.

"Girl, that money is not going to last forever. Especially the way you're spending it. She put their dishes in the sink and headed toward the door. "We'll holla at you later.

Chapter 10

Ten months later ...

"I don't believe this. How does somebody go through two hundred thousand dollars in less than a year?" Tameka asked. "What were you thinking?"

"Don't act like y'all bitches didn't reap some of the benefits. Shit happens. That's all I can say. I feel stupid about blowing all that money, but at the same time I feel relieved," Keisha confessed.

"Yeah, Ms. Relieved, all that is understandable, but how do you plan on paying your bills?"

"I'll get it," Keisha said nonchalantly, rolling her eyes.

"How?" Tameka probed, trying to eat her shrimp and noodles with chopsticks.

Sherrie grabbed a shrimp from Tameka's plate. "She can get a job."

"What job is she going to get paying her enough to cover all her expenses?"

"Sherrie, she's right. Working isn't for me. They work

you like a slave for a few dollars an hour and you have to put up with the exec's funky-ass attitudes and bullshit. Sherman had gotten me a job working with his company, remember? That didn't last longer then a month. My supervisor was jealous of my flavor, always critiquing my clothes and bags. I had to drop my Gucci receipt in front of her one day to let the insecure bitch know that I only rock the real shit."

Sherrie laughed, choking on her food.

"Keisha, you're silly," Tameka said, thumping Sherrie on the back. "Did you drop the receipt for real?"

"I most certainly did. A co-worker told me that she was hating on me. Here I was, admiring the bitch for being the only black woman there with rank and she was secretly stabbing me in the back in the staff meetings. They didn't pay me enough to put up with her. But seriously," she said, slumping back in her chair. "I'm out here living like I'm Queen B for real and now I'm fucked. I didn't do any investing and the little I have left is running out quick."

"What about the money you put up for your mom?" Tameka asked.

"I can't touch that. Only she can and she doesn't know about it."

"Maybe when she gets released from rehab she'll loan you some."

"Girl, are you crazy? I don't want her money. I gave her that so that she won't be coming around me begging. Let her have that shit. She earned it, literally."

"Keisha, do you ever plan on forgiving her?" Sherrie asked.

"I did, with fifty Gs."

Sherrie frowned. "Girl, you know what I mean."

Irritated, Keisha fidgeted in her seat. She didn't like talking or thinking about her mother. She was still hurt by her betrayal. "I don't know, okay? Let's leave it alone and get back to the problem at hand. I need money," she said, dumping the last of the food from the carton onto her plate.

"Downgrade your car," Tameka suggested.

"Hell no. You can't be serious. I can't do that."

"Why?" Sherrie asked, confused. "That's a great idea."

"Because I don't want to. Okay?"

"Hell, you gonna have to give up something," Tameka said.

"Or you can come hit the block with us. We can take the game over. With your brains, Tameka's street knowledge, and my uh" Sherrie's voice trailed off.

"Yeah, whatever," Tameka said, rolling her eyes.

"Hell, I'm a team player with great customer service skills," Sherrie said, popping a shrimp into her mouth.

"I don't know. That's not me. I wouldn't know the first thing to do or say," Keisha said, putting down her fork. She was losing her appetite with all the talk about getting a job and selling her things.

"We'll teach you," Tameka said, warming to the idea.

"I don't know, y'all. I have to think about that."

"Girl, listen. When your back is against the wall, you gotta do what you gotta do." Tameka smirked. "Or do you plan on meetin' another Dino?"

"No," Keisha said. I vowed to never let a man have that much control over me again."

"Exactly. When a man takes care of you, he thinks you're his property," Tameka said.

Keisha tried to think of other alternatives besides hugging the block, but that seemed to be the only way she could get the money she needed quickly. Downsizing her way of living simply wasn't an option.

"We been out here in this heat since sunrise and I only made thirty lousy-ass dollars," Keisha complained. "This sun is beaming on my face; hell, it feels like my mascara is running. How in the hell am I suppose to pay my bills with this little money? How did I get to this point? I'll probably never see the type of money I had again." She looked down at the rocks in her hand. "This shit sure won't bring it. I can't believe I fucked off that much money that quick. I should have made a budget."

"Hey, Keisha, you better get on your square and stop daydreaming and complaining," Tameka warned her. "Five-O gonna roll up on yo' ass. The money is gone, get over it. It happens to the best. You got old drug lords that was ballin' crazy and now they out here broke and smoking."

"That's different. They got a habit, I don't."

"Oh, but you did and still do. You have a shopping habit. You're a shopaholic. You always have to have the latest and hottest shit to hit the streets. Look at you now, on the block tippin' in some damn stilettos. This is not a runway, Keisha. This is the hood and we're selling something illegal. At any given time, you might have to break out and run from the cops or a gang coming through shooting." Tameka shook her head, annoyed with Keisha's constant grumbling.

"But, the way you are isn't all your fault," Sherrie told Keisha. "Dino created that monster. Now, he's gone and his money is gone and you're starting over. Think of it as going to rehab. And you still have a few good things left."

"Like what, Sherrie?" Keisha asked, unconvinced.

"You still got your car, a fly crib, your clothes, and friends that love you. Most importantly, you have your independence. Most people lose everything."

"I hear you, but I need some real money, real fast. This nickel-and-dime shit isn't for us. We need to come up with a strategy to take this block over, to be the queen-pins in this game. If we're gonna play the field, let's play it right and with a goal in mind. There are way too many people out here on one corner hustling the same product and selling the same exact quality of work. We need a come-up, a *big* one."

"Yeah, we do. I see your vision. Hell, I need me a ride like you and Tameka. I'm tired of walking."

"Heifer, you can't even drive," Tameka said.

"I can learn how," Sherrie snapped.

"Whatever. We take you everywhere you have to go, so when do you walk?"

"When I go to the corner store," Sherrie said, her hands on her hips.

"Bitch, please!" Tameka walked away.

"See, Keisha," Sherrie whispered, "her problem is that she can't think past June's ass. She's head over heels for dude. I don't know what kind of spell he has on her. You know that's his work she got. If she sold her own work like she sells his, she would've been ballin' by now. *He's* her only vision."

"I know. But everybody goes through their love spell. She'll wake up, I did. Who would've ever thought that?"

"Yeah, that's true. I would've never thought that."

Keisha gasped and pushed her.

Sherrie shrugged. "What? I'm just saying. You know Dino had you head-gone. Hell, praying didn't seem to work, so I eventually stopped."

"Sherrie, I stopped praying a long time ago."

Before Sherrie could answer, Tameka yelled for her. "Sherrie, here comes Ms. Monroe."

They called her Ms. Monroe because she looked like the world famous sex symbol, Marilyn Monroe. When she needed to buy, she had her driver bring her through the hood in her shiny black Range Rover. Rocking the latest high-end designers and a blinding six-carat rock on her left hand, she was a bad white bitch and she knew it.

Ms. Monroe opened her door and put one foot out, displaying her red bottoms. "Hello, ladies," she said smiling.

"Hi, Ms. Monroe," Tameka and Sherrie said in unison.

"Do you have something for me, Sherrie?"

"Yes. Your usual, right?"

"You know it, darling. I hope it's better than what you had last time. That batch wasn't shit. It didn't even make me want to fuck my husband," she said, making them all laugh.

"Ms. Monroe, you have to be high in order to have sex with your husband?" Sherrie asked.

"Honey, if you saw that old, wrinkled up, short-dick bastard, you would understand."

Tameka looked surprised. "Don't you love your husband?"

"Baby, love and money do not mix. He keeps me

fabulous with a roof over my head, money in my pocket, and clothes on my back. In return, I keep him happy and stress free." She slipped her money to Sherrie and grabbed her stash. "Ta ta, ladies. I'll see you next week. Be careful out here." She put her shades on and closed the door, motioning her driver to go.

When they'd driven away, Sherrie waved her money at Tameka. "See what kindness can get you?"

Tameka rolled her eyes.

"Why does she come to the middle of the ghetto to cop?" Keisha asked. "You'd think she'd have a personal supplier who drops shit off to her. She has a lot of nerve coming in the hood with that expensive jewelry on. She knows muthafuckas out here starving. I'll tell you, drugs give a dying man strength and a coward courage." She shook her head.

"She comes out here so her husband won't catch her. Why else?" Tameka said.

Keisha rolled her eyes. "All I know is that one day somebody gonna rob her ass. Hell, maybe we should." Her face lit up as she thought about rocking Ms. Monroe's ring on her finger.

"Girl, you crazy." Tameka laughed.

"For real. Whatever we take won't fade her."

Sherrie frowned. "Keisha, cool out. You scaring me with all this nonsense you've been talking lately."

"I'm just tripping, Ms. Monroe seems cool. I like her style. Plus, she did kick us down with some old-school game. Love has nothing to do with money. I like that."

"And she tips me well," Sherrie said, smiling. "She gave me an extra fifty dollars,"

"If that's the case, let me hold something, Sherrie,"

Keisha said.

"You can hold your breath and wait." Sherrie laughed and turned away, dodging when Keisha reached for her. Her smile disappeared. "Heads up, T. Here comes June," she said, seeing his car turn the corner.

June pulled up in his outdated, money green Lexus with gold trim, the car vibrating under the loud bass coming from its speakers.

"I guess that's another one of his cousins with him, huh, Tameka?" Sherrie asked, raising an eyebrow.

Tameka sighed. "I'm tired of this shit."

"What are you gonna do?" Sherrie asked sarcastically.

"Watch and see." She headed toward the car.

June hurried out of the car and pulled her to the side. "Hey, baby girl, what's good?"

She pointed at the female in the passenger seat. "Who's that, June?"

"Who?" June said, stalling.

Tameka crossed her arms under her breast and leaned to one side, staring him in the eyes. "Don't fucking play with me. Who is that bitch in your car?"

"Oh, her. That's my cousin. She ain't never been out south before and asked if she could ride." He laughed. "Baby, I know you don't think I'm stupid enough to bring another chick I'm messin' with around you."

"I would think not. So introduce us." Tameka headed towards the car.

"Why? Everybody know about you and what you mean to me. They know you my boo. Come on back here and let me holla at you," he said, grabbing her arm.

"Okay, *boo*. But first let me go meet your cousin," She

yanked loose from his grip. "Since everybody know me by name, it's only right to have a formal introduction, don't you think?"

"Yeah, baby, but now ain't the time. I'm in a rush. I gotta go drop this package off. You'll meet everybody at my family reunion this Saturday, I promise."

"Girl, his corny-ass is playing you," Sherrie yelled. "I bet that's not his cousin."

"Stay the fuck out of my business," June bellowed.

"In your business? Oh, I'm gonna show you *in your business*." She strutted over to the car.

The girl inside was bobbing her head to the music and chewing gum, running colorful nails through her long, blond weave. When Sherrie knocked, she turned and gave her a stank look before turning down the volume and rolling the window down just enough to talk through.

"What's up?" Blondie asked, blowing a bubble and looking Sherrie up and down.

"Excuse me, I hate to bother you in your jam session, but my girl needs some clarity. Are you June's cousin?"

"His cousin?" The girl chuckled and swung her hair. "No, sweetie, I'm his girl. Why?"

"No reason. Thank you for your time." Sherrie turned and smiled. "Tameka, did you hear that? She said she's his *girl*."

"So you're playing me, June?" Tameka asked, frowning.

"Like Alicia Keys plays the piano," Sherrie said. She started singing, "I keep on fallin' innnnn love—"

"Sherrie, shut up," Keisha yelled from the stoop.

"What? I'm just telling her the truth. We told her about his Casanova, fake Don Juan, wannabe ass over and over again. But, no, she wouldn't listen. She wanted to get mad and argue with us."

Before anyone could say anything else, Tameka stormed over to the car. Sherrie jumped back and watched as she knocked on the window, ordering the girl out of the car. The girl frowned, looking back at June.

Check your man, not the woman, Keisha thought. *Not unless she steps out of line. Until then, she's innocent.*

"Girl, you better get the fuck away from my car," June said, walking over.

Tameka turned to him, shocked. He had never spoken to her that way. She'd never even heard him use profanity at all.

"It's like that, June? You'd rather have her over me? After all I've done for you?

"Tameka, you and your shit-starting friend better get the hell away from my car," he ordered.

You choosin' this Barbie-looking, weave-headed bitch over me?" Tameka asked.

"Who you calling a bitch? You a bitch," the girl shouted through the slightly opened window.

Keisha closed her eyes briefly and shook her head. *Oh, Lord. Why did she say that?*

Tameka balled her fists, reached back and swung with all her strength, hitting June in his temple and knocking him off his feet. Climbing on top of him, she continued to swing, punching him in the face.

Sherrie yanked the car door open, snatched the girl out of the car, and started pounding on her.

Watching the commotion, Keisha's mind whirled. Always thinking of a come-up, she remembered where Tameka had told her June kept his stash. She eased over to the driver's side of his car, looking for what she knew would get them started on the road to ballin'. She found what she was looking for—a small, heavy plastic bag—and took it, putting it in a safe place.

That done, she went to help Tameka, who was still beating the fuck out of June. Sherrie had stopped pummeling the girl, leaving her crumpled on the ground, and joined in on whooping June.

Several guys from the block saw them fighting and ran over to assist. They started hitting June with garbage cans, bricks, bottles, and anything else that was in their reach. Neighborhood guys never liked for neighborhood girls to date outside the hood anyway so, they did their best to send June a message to never return. When they heard police sirens, the guys ran off.

June got up and he and the girl staggered to his car.

While driving off, the girl yelled out the window, "I'll be back, bitches. It's not over!"

"That's what they all say," Sherrie yelled back. "We'll be here." She turned back to Keisha and Tameka, grinning. "Did y'all see that uppercut I hit her with? I told y'all my left hook is mean. It's like Mayweather's right hooks."

"Sherrie, be quiet, please," Tameka said in a low voice. Tears rolled down her cheeks. "I've been a fool. That bastard played me."

"Girl, don't sweat it. It happens to the best of us. You know I know how you feel," Keisha said, wiping the tears off her friend's face.

"I tried telling you," Sherrie said.

"Why does love have to hurt?" Tameka asked.

"I have not a clue. After messing with Dino, I asked myself daily if it is really worth falling in love. The only answer I came up with is no."

"Ladies, don't let one bad experience ruin your chances of meeting the person who's right for you," Sherrie said. "Never give up on love. Look at my mom. She hasn't been with another man since my dad got locked up; for ten years she's been alone, waiting on her husband. She said he's the only man for her. And in two more years, she'll have her husband back. Now *that's* love."

"No, Sherrie, that's called loneliness and horny nights," Keisha said, laughing.

"Keisha, you are stupid," Tameka said, starting to laugh.

Sherrie rolled her eyes. "Whatever, you miserable bitches."

"Girl, you know we're just playing with you. We heard everything you said. In my heart, I know it's true. I'm hurt right now, but I'll never give up on love," Tameka said.

"Thank you," Sherrie said. She looked at Keisha, waiting for her response.

Keisha had lapsed into deep thought, contemplating how to tell them she'd hit June's stash. She didn't know how Tameka would respond.

"Hey, T, you still got June's packs?" she asked.

"Yeah."

"What you got?"

"Four packs."

"Four fifty-packs?"

"Yeah. Why?" Tameka asked suspiciously.

"Let's ball!"

"What the fuck is you talking about, 'let's ball'? Off four packs? That's only two Gs."

"Let's kick this shit off. Take it to the next level, build our empire. Instead of hustling for his ass, hustle for yourself." Keisha got excited, thinking her plan through.

"I feel you. Let's kick it off," Sherrie said.

Keisha smiled. "Guess what?"

"What?" Tameka and Sherrie asked in unison.

"I got him."

"What you mean you *got* him?" Tameka asked. "Got who?"

"I hit June's spot," Keisha clarified.

Tameka stared at her, speechless.

"Whatcha get?" Sherrie asked.

"I don't know. But it looks like a lot."

"Bitch, let's see," Tameka demanded.

"Not out here. Let's go to your house. I don't wanna risk driving to my place and getting pulled over."

Approaching Tameka's building, they saw a crowd forming around the front of it.

"Why in the hell are all these people out here?" Tameka asked her upstairs neighbor.

"Jeff just got killed."

"Ms. Woods son Jeff," Tameka asked.

"Yes, that's him," Old Man Charles confirmed. "It seems like the good ones always goes first. Here you have these young dudes out here that don't treasure their life or no one else's and nothing happens to them. But Jeff was a good boy. A college graduate who comes to visit his mother and take her to the grocery store and he gets gunned down right in front of her eyes. This shit doesn't make no sense, I tell you. Instead of jail, they need to send these gangbangers over there to Iraq to fight in a real war." Leaning on his cane, he turned and walked away, shaking his head.

Continuing toward the building, they heard Jeff's mom screaming at the top of her lungs. "God, why my baby lord? Why my Jeff? He's a good boy." They saw a group of people, including Tameka's mom, doing their best to comfort her.

"Damn, that's messed up." Sherrie said sounding disappointed.

"Why you trippin'? I thought you didn't like him," Tameka said.

"That was part of my gimmick to keep him interested. I was going to give him some … one day."

"Some what?" Keisha asked.

"Some good-good! What you think?" Sherrie frowned. "Now it'll never happen."

Tameka and Keisha burst out laughing.

"Quit playing." Keisha said. "Yo' ass ain't giving up nothin'. You'll die a virgin. I don't know where in the hell you gonna get the ten boys you plan on having from"

"Adoption," Tameka said, continuing to laugh.

"Screw y'all loose-pussy sluts. I'm waiting on the right guy. I refuse to go through the drama and bullshit I've seen y'all experience—ass whoopings and pimping."

Keisha and Tameka stopped laughing.

"Whatever," Tameka snapped. "Wipe your feet on the rug. Be quiet and close the door behind you." she instructed. When they were all in her room, she closed the door. "Come on with the come on."

Keisha pulled a clear plastic, bag from her pants and slammed it down on the table. "Bam, there it is."

Tameka and Sherrie's eyes got big.

Sherrie whistled and sat down. "How much you think that is, Tameka?"

"I don't know for certain, I'm guessing around two pounds. It's damn sure enough to get our weight up around this boy," Tameka said.

Keisha grinned. "That's what I'm talking about," she said, rubbing her hands together. "Money, money, and more money."

"That's what's up," Sherrie agreed.

"This is what we're gonna do: get a scale, weigh this shit up, and have somebody test it to see how strong it is," Tameka proposed. Maybe hit it a little more, then chop this boy up and sell it."

"Are we going to move it as weight?" Keisha asked.

"We can't just get out there and start selling weight. Niggas gonna want a cut," Sherrie said.

"We have to do something. I'm tired of this nickel-and-dime shit; I have bills to pay. Maybe we can sell it as twenties," Keisha suggested.

"That sounds like a plan," Tameka agreed.

Keisha looked at Sherrie. "What about you, Sherrie? What you think?"

Sherrie shrugged. "You know I'm down for whatever."

"A'ight, then. Let's get this shit on the ball first thing

tomorrow. This is the best gift that bastard ever gave me," Tameka said.

"Excuse me, don't you mean the best gift *I* ever gave you?" Keisha said, smirking.

Chapter 11

*E*verything went exactly as they planned and it didn't take as long as Keisha thought it would to get on. Their product sold like hotcakes, everyone was buying it. They weren't worried about heat from the guys, Tameka was dating Big Man—the region—and she had him open.

No one could serve on the block without paying their dues unless they were moving some of his packs. He thought he was fronting Keisha and Sherrie work, when all along, they were selling their shit first, then his. As far as the ladies were concerned, it was double income minus the street tax.

Keisha, Tameka and Sherrie were sitting on the block, watching out for five-o while the young hustlers knocked off their bags and came back to re-up twenties from them.

"We came a long way in four months," Keisha said.

"When you got that fire, it doesn't take long to get on," Tameka said.

"I'm ready to snap out. Let's get some new rides," Keisha suggested. "We've got plenty of money saved. Let's do the damn thing."

"Yeah, let's do that. I want me a Cadillac Escalade," Sherrie said.

"Tomorrow, we go on 63rd and Western and look at a car for you, but I don't know about a big SUV," Tameka said. "Until you get more experience by yourself behind the wheel, I don't want you to kill yourself trying to stunt."

"I don't care, I just need some wheels. Plus, Keisha taught me how to drive. And I did pass the road test."

"Keisha taught you in a car, not a big-ass truck." Suddenly feeling a bit nauseous, Tameka made a face. "I don't feel too good," she said.

"What's wrong with you?"

"Not sure. My stomach been upset for a few days now. I'm calling it a night. I'm going to go take some Pepto Bismol and lay down. I'll holla at y'all tomorrow," Holding her stomach, she walked away.

"We'll come check on you later," Keisha called after her. "Get some rest."

"Tomorrow can't get here fast enough for me," Sherrie said after Tameka left, excited about getting a car.

"Me either. I'll probably just upgrade my car."

"Why you think Tameka been so sick lately? You think she's pregnant? My momma said she dreamed about fish the other day."

"I hope not," Keisha said, looking at her. "There's only one way to know for sure."

Determined to find out if Tameka was pregnant or not, Keisha and Sherrie went to a Walgreens to buy a home pregnancy test. At the store, Keisha bumped into one of Dino's old friends.

"Hey, Miss Lady. How you been doing?" the tall, dark-skinned, medium-built dude asked.

"I've been surviving. I'm sorry, what's your name again? It just totally slipped my mind. "

"Steve."

"That's right, Steve. How have you been?"

"You know me, trying to make a dollar out of fifteen cents." He looked her up and down and raised an eyebrow when he noticed the pregnancy test in her hand. "So how's my man doing?"

"Not sure, I haven't heard from him."

By now, she knew word had gotten out that she'd set Dino up. Deciding to counter his story with her own, she pulled Steve aside, lowered her voice, and thought about something sad to bring tears to her eyes. "You know Dino left me before he got locked up, don't you?" She waited a few seconds for him to reply. He shook his head no. She knew she had him then. "He kicked me out the house, packed my belongings in my car, and told me that he was leaving me for Suzie," she said, wiping her eyes.

Steve was shocked that Keisha knew about Suzie, the Latino chick that used to cook his and Dino's work. Dino used to creep with her.

Keisha had found out about her because Suzie and her friend would call Keisha, telling her every dirty detail of their threesomes. Suzie would tell her how Dino ate one's pussy while the other rode his dick. Before hanging up, she'd say, "Tell me, Keisha, how does my pussy juice taste on Dino's tongue?"

Keisha never told Dino. Her mother had taught her that it was a waste of energy to complain about something you have no control over, especially if you plan on staying. So she'd never mentioned the calls.

Steve swallowed every word, his eyes conveying pity for her. Keisha laid her head on his masculine chest, pretending to be too embarrassed to look at him.

He wrapped his arms around her to console her. "Damn, baby, I'm sorry to hear that. I see that it still bothers you, huh? So, how are you getting by? You still look good." he said, inhaling the scent of her perfume.

"I'm beating the block."

"What?" He couldn't believe that Dino left her out here like that. She'd been his main piece.

"Listen, Keisha, put my number in your phone. Call me, I'll hook you up. You don't have to be out here like this. What is the guy you with now doing for you?"

She sniffed. "I'm single."

Sherrie walked over and handed her a napkin.

"You gotta be messing with somebody, you in here buying a pregnancy test," Steve said, pointing to the box in her hand.

"Oh, no, this is for my friend. I've been celibate since Dino left about a year ago."

Steve thought about how tight and thirsty her pussy had to be for some dick and he was sold. Reaching into his pocket, he pulled out a wad of money. He peeled five hundred dollar bills off top and handed it to her. "Here, take this."

"No, Steve, I can't take your money." "Girl take this, it's nothing and if you need anything else, I mean *anything*, call me, no matter the time." he said, licking his lips.

"Okay, I will."

"A'ight, I'm gonna hold you to that." He gave her a hug and, nodded at Sherrie and left the store.

I guess crying does work, Keisha thought, watching him leave. *Glad I took that acting class as an elective.*

She knew Steve was another version of Dino. She was surprised, however, that it was that easy to get money out him. She'd always thought he was a bit cleverer. She smiled to herself, counting the money.

"Girl, that was the best performance I have seen in all my life." Sherrie said, clapping. "You got me in tears, Encore, encore."

"You are stupid," Keisha said, laughing and putting the money in her purse. "Girl, let's get outta here."

When they got to Tameka's house. Keisha walked into her room, pulled the cover off her, and handed her the bag. "Go piss on this," she told her.

"What the fuck is this?" Tameka asked, upset by the intrusion.

"It's a pregnancy test."

"Girl, I'm not pregnant. I ate some Chinese food the other day," she protested

"Tameka, you've been sick for over a week now. If it was the food, you would've shitted it out by now. Just take the damn test!" Keisha ordered.

"A'ight, give it to me. Yo' ass gonna feel like a damn fool when the results are negative." Tameka snatched the bag out of Keisha's hand and headed to the bathroom.

Sherrie and Keisha paced the hallway, waiting for the results.

"Shit, this is taking a long time," Sherrie said.

"Okay," Tameka said, opening the door and holding

the stick for them to see it.

"Two pink lines," Keisha said.

"What does that mean?" Tameka asked nervously. "Where's the box?"

"It means that you're pregnant. Damn, Tameka. What are you gonna do?" Keisha asked.

Tameka shook her head. "I can't believe this. This ain't the time. Maybe the test is inaccurate."

"Have you missed your period?" Sherrie asked.

"No, not at all, that's why I don't believe it's is right. How can I possibly be pregnant and still have my monthly?" She shrugged. "It don't matter. I'm not keeping it."

"Damn, Tameka, you haven't even given it any thought." Sherrie said

"There's nothing to think about. I'm not ready to have a baby. It's too much of a responsibility and I don't want him or her to grow up without a..." Tameka didn't finish her sentence. She sighed and put the toilet lid down, then sat down and stared at the two lines on the plastic stick. Being pregnant was the last thing she'd expected.

"Whose baby is it, Big Man or June's?" Keisha asked.

Tameka paused, thinking. "It's Big Man's. I haven't been with June in over four months and I can't be that far along."

"Damn, time flies. It seems like just yesterday y'all were together."

"Listen, I know you don't want to hear this," Sherrie said, "but every life deserves a chance. God blessed you with this baby for a reason."

"Sherrie, shut the fuck up! You're right. I don't want to hear that preachy bullshit. This is my baby and I'll do what I want to it."

"Listen to yourself, you sound stupid. That *is* your baby, so why would you want to kill a part of you?"

"Sherrie, this is not the time for you to get religious on us. Don't judge her," Keisha said. "That is exactly why people don't like going to church now—because of people like you passing judgment. Most women have to make this decision at some point in their life whether they are financially stable or not, had consensual or forced sex, or if they're in a happy or unhappy marriage or relationship. Until you come face to face with an issue like this, you don't know how you would respond."

"I'm not judging her. I just think she should at least give it some thought. You girls are the closest thing I have to sisters; I would never judge y'all. We're in this together, through thick and thin."

A few days later, Tameka found out that she couldn't abort the baby. She was too far along and it would risk her own life. Looking at her, no one could tell she was pregnant; she barely had a bump on her stomach.

The late stage of her pregnancy confirmed that it was June's baby for sure, but Tameka told Big Man it was his. He had no reason to doubt her. In his eyes, Tameka was a good girl, a hood nigga's dream chick. She was beautiful, knew how to hustle and fight, and would pull the trigger when needed.

Since he and June had similar features and could pass for brothers, she wasn't worried. Even if the baby came out looking exactly like June, Big Man wouldn't be able to tell it wasn't his.

As planned, the girls got new cars. Keisha up-graded her Benz to a silver Range Rover, Sherrie got a Champagne-colored Escalade with 24-inch chrome wheels, and since Tameka had always liked Keisha's car, she got the same newest C5 model. They had officially reached queen-pin status.

It had become their weekly ritual to chill at the car wash on Saturdays mornings while their car get washed. They'd sit and talk shit with old neighborhood hustlers who had fallen off, listening to stories of how thing were when they had been in the game.

Admiring the wax job on her car, Keisha thought about her life two years ago and how much it had changed. *This is the best feeling in the world*, she thought. *No nigga to answer to, no one telling me how much money to spend, or when I can spend it and what to buy. This feels better than sex. I paid for my own car with my own money.*

She looked over at her Sherrie who was also inspecting her car. "It's a good thing you took those extra driving lessons, Sherrie, or you'd wreck that truck."

"It's no bigger than yours," Sherrie said, defending her ride.

"Yeah, but the difference is that I'm used to driving, riding and shifting big gears," Keisha said, thrusting her hips and smirking.

"You two are crazy," Tameka laughed. "Don't start, Keisha. You know how sensitive she gets when it comes to sex."

Sherrie ignored them and watched the man as he put Armor All on her tires.

"I know, but she left herself open for that," Keisha said, laughing.

Chapter 12

*K*eisha and Sherman sat on her plush sofa in the living room. The TV was on, but instead of watching it, they were discussing their dreams and life plans while he massaged her freshly pedicured feet. All of his plans included Keisha, but none of hers included him. He spoke candidly and eagerly about their future—getting married, having children, moving to a warmer climate, and starting a marketing company together.

Keisha knew that she would eventually open her own business and have its name and logo designed and trademarked. Her business plan had been completed before her junior year in college. But getting married, having children, and leaving Chicago weren't options for her. They weren't even possibilities she'd ever considered, especially having children since she would never be able to bear a child.

Keisha had known that his feelings for her were much stronger than her feelings for him. Although she enjoyed his company—mostly his sex—she couldn't allow herself to give away that part of her again. That was one of the reasons she'd never told Tameka and Sherrie about her rendezvous with him. She knew they would encourage her to have more than just a sexual relationship.

As he placed her toes in his mouth and started gently sucking them, her phone rang.

"Um, baby, that feels good," Keisha, whispered, breathing hard.

Her cell phone kept ringing. She reached for it, but Sherman grabbed her hand and held it. "Don't answer it, baby, let it ring."

"I have to, it's Sherrie." She knew by the ring tone. As tempting as he was, Keisha stuck with her promise to always put her money and her best friends before anything else. "What's up, Sherrie?" she answered, trying to control her breathing.

"Tameka is at the University of Chicago Hospital."

"What? What's wrong?" Keisha asked, pulling her foot out of Sherman's mouth and standing up.

"It's the baby."

"I'm on my way!" Grabbing Sherman's things, she escorted him to the door. "Sorry, Sherman, I have to leave. I'll call you later."

Confused, shirtless, and in his boxers, he stood at the door confused. Keisha kissed him quickly on the lips and closed the door before he could speak.

When Keisha arrived at the hospital, she immediately spotted Sherrie on her knees in front of a chair, praying.

"Sherrie, where's Tameka?" she asked.

Sherrie stood up with tears in her eyes and hugged Keisha tightly. From the greeting, Keisha assumed something had happened to the baby or, worse, Tameka. She would be disappointed about not being a godmother, but she wasn't at all emotionally equipped to handle anything happening to one of her best friends. Nervous, she asked Sherrie again where Tameka was.

"She's down the hall. She had the baby. It's a boy."

"What? It's too soon. She's only seven months. Sherrie, please tell me that they are okay?"

"Tameka is fine."

"Oh boy, that's a relief" She took a deep breath. "And the baby?"

"He isn't doing so well; that's why I was praying. Tameka is scared and upset, so act normal when you see her."

After going to the ladies' room to compose themselves, the two of them went to Tameka's room.

"Hey, a boy!" Keisha hollered when they walked in. "Now we have our king," she said, bending down to kiss Tameka's cheek.

"Yeah, if he lives." Tears pooled in Tameka's eyes.

"What do you mean 'if he lives'?" Keisha asked, frowning.

"He's premature. The doctor said it don't look too good. I should've gone for prenatal care," Tameka said, crying.

"Tameka, he's going to be just fine. He comes from a team of fighters. He'll survive, I'm sure of it. There's not a doubt in my mind and there shouldn't be one in yours." Keisha said.

"Yes, Tameka, we all are praying for his victory," Sherrie said. "Matthew 18:20 states, 'For where two or three are gathered together in my name, there am I in the midst of them.' Jesus hears our prayers and he is here and we know how he likes to show up and show out.

Tameka sniffed. "I hope he survives. I finally got somebody to love me for me. You know what I mean?"

Sherrie picked up her hand and held it. "We love you."

"I know, but I got a man to love me now. That's what I've always wanted."

Keisha and Sherrie knew growing up without knowing who her father was bothered Tameka, but they'd had no idea to what extent it had affected her.

Keisha tried to lighten the mood. "What are you going to name him?"

"Emonie," Tameka said.

"That's unique. I like it. Yeah, it rhymes with money. I like it a lot," Keisha said.

"Bitch, you stupid," Tameka said, laughing. "You're going to make me bust my stitches."

Pleased to see a smile on her face, Keisha and Sherrie continued telling jokes to keep her mind occupied. They stayed until visiting hours were over and left with promises to return the next day.

Sherrie and Keisha handled all the business. Afterward, they'd go to the hospital to keep Tameka updated on what was happening in the streets and to check on their godson.

Arriving for the daily visit three weeks later, Keisha and Sherrie found Tameka standing outside her room, talking to the doctor. He said that Emonie was doing much better than they'd expected, but he wouldn't be able to go home for another week. They wanted to keep a close eye on him. He did, however, sign Tameka's release papers. She was cleared to go home.

"Tameka, you need to rest," Keisha told her. "Look at you, you have bags under your eyes. If you keep stressing like this, your hair will start thinning, or worse, falling out. Let's take a trip before the baby comes home. You need to relax and get your mind right."

Sherrie agreed. "Yeah, Tameka, you need a break. We can get your mother and my mother to take turns staying up here with Emonie."

"Are you bitches crazy? I can't leave my baby, he needs me."

"It's just for the weekend, Tameka, Keisha said. "You'll come back with a peace of mind and you'll be rested. My cousin told me about a big event they're having in Cancun this weekend."

"Cancun?" Tameka and Sherrie said in unison.

"Yeah! He said everybody who's somebody will be out there, mostly all the hip-hop celebrities. Plus, I heard they have some beautiful beaches."

"That does sound like fun and I do need a vacation. I've never been on one before. But I can't leave my son and my body isn't beach-ready. " Tameka complained.

"Girl, please, you'll look fine after a facial and a pair of Spanx," Keisha told her. "You will look amazing. We'll just lounge around the pool and soak up the sun."

"Won't it be expensive to get the tickets at the last minute?" Tameka asked.

" My cousin got a hook up. He's gonna get them for us."

"Okay, then. I guess I'll go. I do need the rest before the baby come home," Tameka said.

"I'm in too," Sherrie said.

Keisha pumped a fist in the air. "Cancun, here we

come!"

Chapter 13

*E*xiting the airplane and walking toward the luggage area, they were excited to be in Cancun, but even more excited to have their feet touching land.

"Hey, are y'all ears ringing?" Keisha asked.

"Yeah, mine are," Tameka said, rubbing her temples. "My head hurt more from listening to Sherrie with all her praying, though."

"I was scared to death," Sherrie said. "The noise from the engine and the turbulence made it hard for me to relax. I should have never taken a flight that long, considering this was my first time flying. I'm sorry if my praying bothered y'all, but that's what I do when I'm nervous."

Keisha shook her head. "Girl, we told you to have a drink. It would've calmed your nerves."

After getting their bags, the girls strutted through the airport like they were models on a runway. They proceeded outside to wait for Andre.

Andre picked them up from the airport and drove them straight to the hotel. Their eyes were glued to the windows, admiring the *white sand beaches* caressed by turquoise waters. They couldn't believe how beautiful it was.

Pulling into the parking lot of the Royal Hotel where they would be staying for the next couple of days, they saw people everywhere. Loud hip-hop music blasted and girls gyrated to the beat while the fellas watched, admiring their string bikinis.

"Wow, it's a lot of people here," Sherrie said, looking around as they walked toward the hotel doors.

Andre laughed. "Yeah, mostly horny-ass niggas and gold-diggin' bitches selling pussy. Y'all can come up out here."

"Sorry, but I don't sell sex," Sherrie said, insulted by his implication.

Andre looked at her. "Did I say that? You don't have to sell shit. A promise gets you more, anyway. Tease a nigga, make him think he got a shot at getting in that ass. Trust me, he'll do whatever you ask *and* what you don't ask."

"So niggas out here with that bag?" Keisha asked.

"Yeah. You know muthafuckas like to front. Niggas out here with their life savings, trying to keep up with these studio gangsters."

Keisha thought about what he said. She wanted to buy a $2,500 Louis Vuitton bag she'd seen at Neiman Marcus with a matching diaper bag to carry for when she'd have Emonie.

"Cuz, so you saying that I can just tease one of these cats and get paid?" she inquired.

"What part didn't you understand? Listen, y'all some bad bitches, and I say that with the utmost respect. I'm not gonna front; any dude would be happy to be seen with y'all. Just look how these niggas looking at me now. They probably think I'm a pimp. It's up to y'all to get this money out here. Take this," he instructed, handing Keisha a small bottle that look like eye drops.

"What's this?"

"Just put a few drops in a nigga's drink. I guarantee he'll pass out in two minutes. Oh, here's some spending money and your room key. Call me when y'all get dressed. I'm outta here." He turned and walked toward the elevators.

The girls looked at each other, stunned. Their plans were to come out to Cancun and enjoy themselves, not hustle.

"I don't know about that, Keisha," Tameka said. "I'm usually down for whatever, but ripping niggas off comes with consequences,"

"I feel you, Tameka," Sherrie said, agreeing.

"What consequences?" Keisha gestured to the people around them. "These fools out here don't know us from the man on the moon. This will be a quick come-up. And if anything go down, Andre out here with his boys and, trust me, he got my back for sure."

Tameka and Sherrie exchanged a look, unconvinced.

"Sherrie, you said you wanted to move out of your mama's crib and, Tameka, you just had Emonie. We can use the extra cash."

Tameka looked at Sherrie. "She does have a point."

Sherrie paused. "A'ight, let's do it, but only one time. After that, we on the first flight outta here. You two money-hungry heifers are gonna be the death of me."

"I knew y'all would come around. Since we're doing this only once, we have to make it count." Keisha said.

After going to their room and unpacking, they decided to go hang out at Cancun Beach Bar and enjoy the Caribbean breeze while sipping margaritas.

"Every hip-hop star you can name is out here," Sherrie said. "I've seen T.I, Lil' Wayne, 50 cent, Luda, and P. Diddy. Security won't let anybody close to any of them, though. I want to see my girls, Trina and Rihanna."

"Stars? They ain't no damn stars. Stars are in the sky. These muthafuckas are just people nationally and internationally known, like we're going to be. Well-known queen-pins," Keisha lifted her glass in a toast.

Sherrie shook her head. "Something is wrong with you, Keisha. You changed."

"Girl, everybody changes, don't they?" She sat back in her chair. "Some for the better, others for the worse. I just got a bit of both."

"I agree with Sherrie, your ass is crazy now. But, I like the new you. The new you keeps all our pockets fat." Tameka laughed.

"Okay, I'll take that. One thing that will never change about me is the love I have for y'all, my sistas. Let's make a toast to freedom, friendship, loyalty, and money."

"Cheers," they all said.

Keisha worked the room with her eyes. Spotting their victims, she smiled. Baby-ballers—young niggas with money.

"Ladies, let's go sit at the bar," she said.

As they walked by the group of guys, she gave a tall, handsome guy a welcoming, seductive smile. As she expected, he pursued her.

"Excuse me, Ma," he said, gently grabbing her arm and pulling her back towards him.

He's aggressive. Keisha thought.

"Yes?"

"Can I talk to you for a minute?"

"Sure." Keisha waved for her girls to come back. They walked with him over to where his boys were standing. "Hello, fellas, what are you guys up to?"

A light-skinned brother with a mohawk looked them up and down. "Nothing, what's up with y'all?"

"We can't call it. Where are you guys from?"

"South Carolina, shawty."

"A'ight. You from the dirty-dirty," Keisha joked.

"No doubt. Where y'all beauties from?"

She thought quickly. "L.A."

"Y'all don't act like no L.A. chicks," Light-skinned said.

"How do L.A. chicks act?" Tameka asked.

"Normally, y'all L.A. chicks are stuck-up."

"I don't know about the other L.A. ladies, but we're down to earth," Sherrie told him.

"Yeah, we all came out here to have a good time, right?" Keisha said. "No need to act funky and stank. Let's enjoy each other's company. Ya feel me?"

The group laughed at her attempt to sound southern.

"I dig that, Ma. Why don't y'all come to our room later to sip on a little something and cheef? We can host our own party. Ya feel me? I got some bottles of Moet and some weed that will make you fall back better than that Cali shit."

"That's cool. What hotel are y'all staying at?" Keisha asked.

"We're at the Hilton, suite three-one-two. By the way, my name is Buck."

"Buck?" Tameka said.

"Yeah."

"Why they call you Buck?"

He bit his bottom lip and grabbed his crotch. "'Cause I get them bucks all day and all night. Ya heard me?"

Keisha, Tameka and Sherrie bit back chuckles.

"Oh, I like that name, Buck." Keisha blushed.

Tameka eyed the dark dude in the group. "We'll see y'all later."

That nigga is a clown. Hmmm, 312 is our area code. That has to be a sign, Keisha thought as they walked away.

Back at the hotel, they put on the skimpiest outfits they had. Sherrie slipped into a form-fitting, white, open-front, backless mini dress that displayed her voluptuous breast, small waist, ample behind, and toned thighs. She accessorized it with gold jewelry and strappy Michael Kors sandals that Keisha had bought her from Sincere's boutique. Tameka wore a cream and black fitted dress that hugged her curves and a pair of black open toe shoes. Keisha pranced in front of the mirror, wearing a two-piece dress with a sheer bottom that revealed her boy cut undies, flat stomach, and long legs. She topped it off with studded, open-toe Louboutins.

"I must admit, we look like the best of the best video vixens," Sherrie said. "Just think, last year we didn't even know that this shit existed. We've come a long way."

Keisha nodded in agreement. "You're right, Sherrie, we did. Now, let's go hit these fools' pockets. I called Andre and let him know where we'll be, just in case anything pop off. The plan is to tease, drug, then rip their asses off."

"Let's roll," Tameka said.

Reaching the guys' hotel, they saw a lot of chicks in the lobby. One girl was damn near naked, walking around the lobby in a G-string and bikini top. Keisha spotted her cousin with a chick on his lap and an interesting-looking older fellow sitting next to him.

Andre held his glass up to her in acknowledgement. She smiled and continued toward the elevators. The doors opened and their mouths dropped open. A girl was giving a heavy-set guy a blowjob in the elevator. Dude smirked at them before reaching over and pressing the button to close the door.

"I swear, some people don't have any class," Sherrie said.

"See, hoes like them make bitches like us look bad," Tameka said. "It's not what you do, it's how you do it."

Keisha frowned in disgust. "Well, I hope he's paying like he weigh, because that was just nasty. It looked like she had to hold up his belly to get to his dick."

Tameka laughed. "Keisha, you are stupid."

Taking the stairs wasn't an option for them in their heels, so they waited patiently for the next elevator to arrive, hoping they wouldn't be treated to another up-close dick-sucking demonstration. The next one was empty.

Inside it, Sherrie turned up her nose. "Make sure not to lean on anything in here. You'll mess around and catch the heebie jeebies."

"What the hell is 'the heebie jeebies,' Sherrie?" Keisha asked.

"Not sure, but I heard that it's something you can't get rid of."

"Girl, there's no such thing" Tameka told her. "Stay off that damn internet. It's gonna fuck your mind up."

When they got to the right floor, they stepped off the elevator and walked down the hall, looking for the the room number. Approaching a room with food trays and empty pizza boxes in front of the door, they could smell the heavy aroma of marijuana.

"Here's the room right here," Tameka said.

Before she got a chance to knock on the door, a short, chunky dude opened it and greeted them. "Damn, y'all look gooder than a muthafucka," he said, licking his lips. "Very tasty, I mean sexy."

"We know," Keisha said, winking at him when they walked past him.

"Where's the music?" Sherrie asked.

He pointed to a stereo sitting on the table.

She went over, turned the volume up high, and started to dance, teasing with her every move.

I guess watching those music videos paid off, Keisha thought, watching her.

Sherrie had a bad-ass body and she knew it. She loved her Coke bottle shape. It was her badge of honor. Her body, she often said, was her temple. That's why she refused to give it to any guy who wasn't ready to make her an honest woman.

While all eyes were on Sherrie, Keisha fixed drinks for her, Tameka and Sherrie. After making sure no one was watching, she slipped the stuff Andre gave her into the bottle and went around the room, pouring it into cups the guys were already drinking out of. Ten minutes later, Sherrie was still working it and two guys were dancing on her.

Tameka was cheating two others with trick dice she'd brought from home, watching what they were working with and where they pulled their stash from. They were playing for pussy and head, she was playing for Benjamin's.

Never one to pass up an opportunity to get her kitty pampered, Keisha had the tall guy in the corner going down on her. She poured champagne between her breasts, letting it flow down her stomach and to her pussy, where he sucked it all up.

Looking over at Sherrie, she saw her giving one of the guys she'd been dancing with a lap dance. He stroked her breasts while she gyrated on him. Both were so into it, they didn't notice the other guy had passed out and was on the floor.

I guess that's how she can maintain her virginity, Keisha thought. *She just grinds herself into a climax. Go 'head, girl, get your rocks off.*

While she watched, the young boy reached his climax and then he, too, was knocked out. She turned toward Tameka and saw the two dudes she'd been gambling with were also now on the floor.

Realizing she didn't feel any movement in her southern region, she looked down. "Damn, I didn't even cum yet." She sighed." Oh well, time to do what we came to do."

The girls hit every drawer and suitcase in the room. Knowing how guys in the hood had a habit of hiding shit on themselves, they also checked pockets, socks, and caps too. They got away with twenty thousand dollars and some jewelry.

Back in their room, Tameka called home to check on Emonie. Her mother told her that he was being released from the hospital the next day.

Keisha hooked up with Andre the next morning at breakfast. He introduced her to John, the older man he was with the night before. The two exchanged numbers and she and the girls headed for the airport.

They wanted to make sure they were back in Chi-town when the king of their dynasty came home.

Chapter 14

ack home, Keisha called Sherman.

"Hello?"

"Hey, baby," she purred. "What's up with you? I miss you."

"Nothing much," he responded, sounding nonchalant.

Keisha frowned at his tone. "Why you sound so dry? Don't you miss your baby?"

"Listen, Keisha, I can't play this game with you any longer. I don't want to be just your sex buddy; I want to be your man, your provider, the one you come to in your time of need. I want to be your *husband*, Keisha. When I look at you, all I see is the lady I want to spend the rest of my life with. Unfortunately for me, you don't feel the same."

Keisha held the phone, speechless.

"Keisha? Are you still there?"

"Yes, I'm still here."

"Do you have anything to say?"

Keisha knew that she couldn't give him what he wanted. Although she had feelings for him, they weren't the same as his. *If I can get him to come over, I can at least get some of his good-good one last time.*

"Oh, uh ... Sherman, this conversation is a bit much for me right now. I just got off a three-hour flight and I have jet lag. Why don't you come over and help me unwind? We'll talk more about it when you get here."

"I'm not coming over there. I'm not your boy-toy Keisha. I have to go. Call me when you're ready to settle down." The line went silent.

"Hello? Hello? Sherman? Sherman!" Keisha looked at her phone and saw that he had hung up.

Keisha paced back and forth, arguing with herself, wondering if she was making a mistake by letting him go.

Damn, Keisha, what have you done? Sherman is a good man, he's not like Dino. He would be a good provider.

No, fuck that. Dino was a good provider, but remember the ass kickings that came along with it?

She decided it was best for them to go their separate ways. She just wasn't emotionally capable of giving him the love he deserved.

Bored and scrolling through her phone, Keisha came across John's number. He was older, but a very attractive man. He looked like a black Sean Connery. According to Andre, John was as big as they got. Keisha had figured that out just by his presence. She had been around men with money all her life, so she recognized niggas with money and power when she saw them. The way they moved and spoke was very different from the ones who had short or new money.

When she called him, John invited her and her girls to a party he was having at his house in Olympia Fields. She knew there would be a swarm of girls there vying for his attention and praying that he'd choose them. Even if it was only for that one night, they'd prance around, hoping to make a few bucks or that they'd impress him enough sexually to knock his wifey out of place or become his side piece of the month.

Keisha loved to shut hoes like that down. She knew that when she, Tameka and Sherrie walked into a room, men as well as women paused. Ready for a challenge, she rounded up the girls and they got dressed and headed to the party.

They arrived at a white mini-mansion flanked by two lion's statues on each side. The gold and brass double doors opened and they stepped into what seemed more like an orgy than a party. The staff of all women servers wore nothing but thongs. They saw two girls going at it hard on the black leather sofa. In another room, a short midget with a patch over one eye was overseeing a dick-sucking contest.

"Whoever make one of these niggas cum in under five minutes will walk away with a stack," he yelled.

The line of women for the contest reached outside the

living room and into the kitchen.

"Keisha, where in the hell is dude?" Sherrie asked. She was uncomfortable.

"Yeah, I'm about to leave," Tameka said. "This is some bullshit. What the fuck does he think? That we're gonna get down like this?"

Sherrie frowned and crossed her arms. "I hope not. He'll be sadly mistaken."

"Hello, ladies" John said, walking up and extending his arms to welcome them.

"So, this is how the rich party?" Keisha asked.

"No, this is just a little something we do to unwind." He looked at her, admiring the way her formed-fitted dress hugged her curves.

She rolled her eyes. "We don't get down like this."

"I'm sure you don't. I just wanted to meet the ghetto beauties and introduce you all to my world. Your cousin told me a lot of good things about you. Let's go into my office."

The girls followed him down the hall and into another room. John closed the door and leaned on his marble top desk. He grabbed a cigar from the humidor on his desk and offered them one, they refused. After lighting one for himself, he looked at them.

"I have a proposition for you ladies. How would you like to leave that petty hustling alone and make some real money?"

"What do you have in mind?" Keisha asked. Andre

didn't know about her beating the block, so she didn't have a clue as to what he had told John about her.

"Listen, I'm going to get straight to the point. I got a few people who owe me some money. I need them to be taken care of discretely."

"You want us to kill people who owe you money," Keisha asked, incredulous.

John stared at her without blinking. "No and yes. I want you to bring them to their final destination; my guys will take care of the rest. Do you think you're capable of handling that?"

Keisha turned her head. His stare was making her uncomfortable.

"If you kill them, then you'll never get your money back," Sherrie said.

John smirked as he turned to look at her. "Baby girl, it's not about the money for me, it's the principle."

"We have to think about this," Keisha said.

"It pays well. You get ten percent of what they owe me. And they don't go on the list for anything less than fifty grand."

Keisha did the math in her head. She looked at Tameka and Sherrie before turning back to John. "So, we get a minimum of five Gs for setting a nigga up?"

"That's right." He knew that money was what turned Keisha on. Looking at her, he could tell that she was accustomed to the finer things in life.

"What if something jumps off before your guys arrive

and we have to shoot them?" Tameka asked. "We've never taken someone's life before."

Keisha was silent, remembering Reggie. She'd never regretted what she'd done that night.

"And you won't have to," John said. "Talk it over and let me know what y'all decide. Keep in mind that two of my guys will always be there. You will never know who they are, but they will know who you are. I know you three have it in you. Cancun was a test and y'all passed." He stood and escorted them outside to their car.

Smiling, he kissed each of their hands. "Let me know something within forty-eight hours. Enjoy your night, ladies."

Although they knew a lot of dough was involved and it was easy money, they all had much more to lose if word got out—their lives.

Keisha's phone rang before six the next morning. It was Tameka.

"Let's do it," she said simply.

"What?" Keisha asked. "Are you sure?"

"Yeah. We're not gonna let anything happen to each other or Emonie, and Big Man would die protecting Emonie and me.

"Are you sure you want to do this, though?"

"Yeah."

Keisha was silent for a moment. "Well, I guess it's on."

"I'll call Sherrie and tell her that we're gonna do it. I

know she'll be down. We can all save enough money to get the fuck out the hood and leave this street shit alone forever. With this hustle and our work, we'll be completely out before you know it."

"True. Plus, I'm ready to start my marketing company and this money sure as hell will help."

"Girl, your marketing company is gonna be the bomb. Look how you strategized our hustle, now we all eatin'."

Keisha heard the baby crying in the background. "Is that Emonie?"

"Yeah, he's hungry."

"Girl go feed my Godson. I need to get some sleep anyway. I'll call you later. Peace."

"Peace."

Keisha called Andre and told him what they'd decided.

"I knew you would, cuz. And you know I wouldn't let you get into this if I thought it was too dangerous. I wouldn't get my fam hurt. My girl, Tabitha, used to do it."

He broke the news to her that he had to turn himself in the next day to do three years. He'd been fighting a case for several years. They tried to give him twenty-five years to life for manslaughter, but John had hired the best criminal lawyer in Chicago for him and they'd worked out a plea agreement for a lesser charge and smaller sentence.

Keisha was sad and now hesitant about working for

John.

"Maybe we shouldn't do this then, Andre. I agreed because I knew you'd have my back. I don't know John like that."

"He's like a father to me, cuz, and I trust him with my life. He'll protect you and make sure you're straight financially. I told him to look after you while I'm gone."

"So, will I see you before you turn yourself in?" Keisha asked with tears in her eyes.

"For sure. I'll stop by later." She heard a beep. "I have to take this other call. Love ya, cuz."

"Love ya more, Andre. I'm glad we linked back up. It feels good to be around blood."

"I know the feeling. I'll see ya later."

"A'ight."

Keisha laid back on her bed, unable to hold back her tears. She knew she still had Tameka and Sherrie, but she felt alone. Her security blanket was gone for three years. She knew she had to toughen up to survive the deadly chaos of the streets long enough to save enough money to get out and start her company.

Chapter 15

*K*eisha wasn't able to see Andre before he turned himself in. She did speak to him again, though, and he told her that he didn't like to have any contact with the outside world while locked up. He had to maintain a prison mentally to deal with the convicts in there; he couldn't be distracted by what was going on in the outside world. She didn't understand his method of surviving in prison, but she didn't question it.

She went on with the original plan and met up with John, letting him know they were accepting his job offer.

He had his boys take them out on his shooting range. They were taught how to properly hold a gun, aim it, and shoot it. They learned on every gun he thought they could handle, among them, a Dillinger, .22, .45, and a nine.

"Damn, this feels good," Tameka said. "Every time I pull the trigger, I get this strong, satisfying feeling."

Keisha laughed. "I know the feeling. It's called power."

"Yeah, power. That's exactly what it feels like." She took aim at their target—a cardboard replica of a police officer—and fired repeatedly, each shot hitting the spot she'd aimed for.

It wasn't a secret that John hated Chicago's finest. He compared them to the Mafia, saying that they were the worst and most dangerous gang on the streets. They knew the law and how to get around it.

"Their badges are a symbol that they can steal, kill, and destroy without any consequences," he said. "Police officers can do whatever the hell they feel like and there's not much you can do about it in the streets, not unless you're as equally powerful."

A cop had killed his identical twin brother, James, when they were sixteen. The two boys had just left basketball practice at Phillips High School and were walking home when they heard a woman in the alley screaming.

"Somebody help me, please!"

Without hesitation, not thinking about their own safety, they ran to help.

They saw the lady lying on her stomach, completely naked, stretched out on the filthy pavement with her hands and feet tied behind her back. Shocked, they had stood there, frozen at the sight.

"Untie me, please. Help me before he comes back to kill me," she had begged.

James tried to untie the knot, but he was unsuccessful. He'd told John to find a piece of glass or something sharp for them to cut her loose. When they managed to free her, she stood up and they got a full view of her body. It was the first time either of them had seen a naked woman other than the ones that were in their father's Playboy magazine. Those ladies, however, couldn't compare to what was in front of them.

A beautiful, curvy, black woman with her long hair pulled back in a ponytail stood in front of them. They admired her perky, pear-shaped breasts, small waist, and wide hips before snapping back to reality. James gave her his jacket to cover herself.

"Thank you, boys, for helping me," she said.

A police officer pulled up and jumped out with his gun drawn. "Let her go," the white police officer shouted, pointing his gun at James.

Both boys got scared.

"Sir, we were helping her," James tried to explain nervously.

"Let her go," the officer said again. This time, his voice was more forceful, deeper and conveying more authority.

James stepped away from the lady and bent down to pick up his backpack. That's when the officer shot him.

John ran to his brother's side.

His brother was gasping for air.

"Help me, help me," John screamed at the lady, tears running down his face.

She took off running.

The officer walked over to John with his gun pointed at him. He picked up the backpack and opened it. All he'd found were some books, a basketball, and a pair of gym shoes. He then ran to his car and called for help. It took the ambulance ten minutes to arrive. James was pronounced dead on arrival at the hospital. The officer had shot him in his chest and the bullet had struck his heart.

Their parents had done everything in their power to have the officer fired and had sued the Chicago Police Department for first-degree murder of their son. In court, he claimed that James had pulled a gun on him and that he shot him in self-defense. It had been the white police officers word against John's, a young black kid from the

Ida B. Wells projects. Without any other witnesses, they didn't have a chance. John never saw the lady that they helped again and, even with all the media coverage the case received, she never came forward.

The police officer had gotten off and was reinstated. John was devastated, his faith in the judicial system gone. His hatred for the white officer had grown each day that passed. He followed the officer for years, observing his habits and daily routine.

On John's twenty-first birthday, as a gift to his brother, he went to the officer's house and threw a cherry bomb through the window, killing the officer's wife and new-born son. The next day, the officer was on the news pleading for whoever killed his wife and son to come forward.

John knew the pain that he saw in the officer's eyes very well. It was the same pain he, his mother, and his father would carry for the rest of their lives. He'd sat in front of the TV, raised a glass of champagne in the air, and wished his deceased brother a happy birthday.

After weeks of watching the girls practice and evolve into the devious bitches he knew they really were, John was ready to put them to work.

"Ladies, it's time," he said.

Their first assignment was to set up a dude named Michael in Detroit. He was originally from Chicago, but had moved to Detroit to lay low after the cops raided his spot, causing him to go into debt with John for $60,000.

John had given Michael a year to pay the money back. It had now been two years and not once had he attempted to make a payment toward his debt., Not only that, but he'd changed his phone number to avoid contact with John. Now, he was on the list. Since John had never sent a message for his money after the first year, Michael assumed that the loss had been charged to the game and had started coming to Chicago every weekend to check on his new spot.

John and his boys had watched him for three weekends straight, getting familiar with where he went and what he did, looking for his weaknesses. Like most men, it was pussy. He had to have a new chick in his bed every weekend. Not just any chick, though. His type was a thick chick with a caramel complexion, naturally long hair, and long legs—girls that looked like Keisha.

Friday morning, Keisha went to her hair stylist, Toccara, a celebrity stylist and the owner of the popular Dazja'Vu salon to get her hair straightened. She didn't have to worry about Toccara prying in her business like the other nosey stylists. She was always in and out of there in a timely manner.

Keisha had never liked the salon setting, with girls there telling all their business and fighting and arguing over a dick that none of them could control. She always made her appointments for early morning so she could avoid all that.

After the salon, she treated herself to the spa. She was starting to tense up from nervousness and needed to relax. Hours later, she sat in her room staring at the picture of her and her father, wondering if he was disappointed in her.

"Daddy, I promise to make you proud," she said aloud. "I'm going to change my life around as soon as I make enough money."

She walked to the kitchen and poured herself a glass of red wine, then flipped through her mail before heading to her bedroom to get dressed.

She dressed in what she called her "Freakum dress".

The dress guaranteed to get her a buyer. It was a lace mini-dress with sheer lace paneling that exposed her back. Its low cut front gave a preview of her perfectly-shaped breasts. Sincere had given her the dress for her twenty-first birthday as a way of welcoming her into adulthood. She slid her feet into four-inch, multi-colored, snakeskin Gucci peep toe pumps and took one last look in the mirror. The words to Tweet's song came to her— *There goes my hand all over myself, oh my.*

Keisha wished Sherman could see her. She missed him, not just the amazing sex, but also the time they'd spent together laughing, talking about their life dreams, rapping, dancing, and joking. But her pride, pain, and stubbornness wouldn't allow her to submit to his requirement.

I'll bump into him one day, she thought. *Chicago isn't that big and, when I do see him, I'll be looking so good he won't be able to resist. Then the ball will be back in my court.*

Michael's club was in a secluded area on the north side of Chicago. When Keisha, Tameka, and Sherrie walked in, he was sitting in the VIP section, watching the dance floor.

They moved through the crowd of females in skimpy dresses, positioning themselves in his view, and started dancing seductively under the soft lighting, making sure that he got a clear view of Keisha. She moved her body like a snake while rubbing her hands up and down her hips and thighs, dipping low and rolling back up, lightly tapping her round ass as she moved her hips from side to side. She ran her fingers through her hair, softly biting on her bottom lip.

She was duplicating Sherrie's moves from Cancun. Pleased, Sherrie smiled at her.

Michael watched her hips sway, fantasizing about what he was going to do to her. He knew he was gonna be swimming in her tonight. She was the chosen one. He waited patiently until they left the dance floor and went to the bar. Then he sent one of his boys over to get her.

Excuse me, miss," the husky dark-skinned guy said. "My man over there would like to meet you and buy you and your friends a drink."

Tell him thank you, but no thanks," Keisha said. "We can afford our own drinks."

She smiled and walked toward the ladies' room, giving him a view of her bodacious rear. She knew men with little money didn't like to be rejected, especially in front of their friends. It hurt their egos.

When she came out of the bathroom, just as she'd planned, Michael was standing there.

"So you want to give a brotha a hard time?" he said, his smile displaying even, pretty, white teeth.

Up close, Keisha saw that he was fine as hell considering he was light-skinned with freckles, which she had never been attracted to. He was six-three and medium-built with a low wavy fade, manicured nails. And he smelled good.

Damn, what a difference a close-up makes.

She smiled and spoke in a seductive voice. "No, brother, I just want the man that's interested in me to approach me."

"Look, Ma, I'm a man who knows what he wants, so I'm going to get right to the point. I enjoyed the way you moved on that dance floor, I like the way you look, your style is fly. I want to see how your inner lips feel. I don't mean any disrespect, I'm just keepin' it one hundred. Now tell me, how much is the bill?"

Cute, Keisha thought, looking into his hazel eyes. "How much are you willing to part with?"

"On the average, I pay three to four hundred. But, since you look like a ride that's sure to please, I'll splurge and give you five hundred."

"Make that a G and we got a deal."

He smiled and said, "A G? You better do some bad-ass tricks."

"You said yourself I look like a ride that's sure to please."

He looked her up and down, admiring her long legs, imagining them wrapped around his waist. He ran his hands through her hair, checking for tracks. Satisfied, he said, "A'ight, cool. A G it is. Let's bounce."

Keisha went and told her girls she was leaving. A nervous-looking Sherrie and Tameka warned her to be careful.

"Call me as soon as you get out," Tameka said.

"You know I will."

Keisha and Michael left for his spot, leaving his crew and her girls at the club. His bachelor pad, just a short drive away, was decked out with a 60-inch flat screen TV, dark, burgundy furniture, and a bear rug in the middle of the floor. Custom window blinds had a picture of Scarface on them

"Take your shoes off, get comfortable. Would you like something to drink?"

"No, thank you. I have to use the bathroom, though. Where is it?"

"Go down the hall and make a right."

"Is someone else here?"

"Naw, baby, just me and you."

Nervous and scared that he knew it was a setup and was setting her up, Keisha looked in each room she passed, making sure no one else was there. Arriving at the bathroom, she slowly pushed the door open.

Damn, if this is his lay low spot, I would love to see where he actually lives, she thought.

She looked around the room, taking in the huge Jacuzzi tub, wall-to-wall mirrors, and his and hers marble sinks.

If he can afford all this shit, how come he can't pay his debt?

Looking in the mirror, she silently coached herself. *Okay, Keisha this is it. It's too late to back out now. Do what you have to do and get out of here alive.*

Michael's voice came from down the hall. "Are you a'ight in there?"

"Yes, here I come." She hurriedly freshened up her kitty and exited the bathroom.

His eyes followed her when she walked back into the living room and crossed the room.

"What are you staring at?" she asked jokingly.

"Stop right there," he said. He went over to a black box on the wall.

Aw shit, this is it. Damn! I fucked up. John told me to keep my piece on me at all times.

She spotted her purse on the glass table and started moving in that direction.

"Didn't I tell you not to move?" he said, smiling.

Thinking quickly, she said, "I need to get my lipstick."

"What for?"

"Well, whenever I'm going to be a nasty girl, I like to put on my red lipstick. It helps me get in character."

"Baby, you don't need that. I'll help you get in character. Plus that shit is hard to wash off my dick. Now, be a good little girl and stand right there. Don't make Daddy spank you."

Did I say this included a blowjob, you cocky bastard? Keisha thought. She stayed silent, trying to think of a way to get to her purse without him getting suspicious.

"Well, Daddy, I got some mints in there. You know the amazing feeling mints will give you when getting a blow job, don't you?"

Michael didn't know, but acted like he did. He was more than eager to find out. "Okay, baby. Go get your mints."

"Thank you, Daddy."

Keisha walked over to her purse, not taking her eyes off Michael, watching his every move. She dug in her bag and was just about to pull her Dillinger out when he waved his hand in front of the black box. The doors opened and he pressed a button. The smooth sound of Sade singing "Cherish the Day" filled the room. Keisha took her hand off her pistol and grabbed a mint instead. *I couldn't have picked a better song myself.*

"Strip for me," he ordered.

"What?"

"Strip for me."

She had never done a strip tease before. Dino hadn't been into that. When she tried to strip for him once, he'd told her he didn't like to be teased, only pleased.

How can I deny a dying man his last wish?

She turned around and put her purse on the table. She slowly bent forward, tipping her apple bottom in the air and giving him a full view. Swiftly, she came back up, flipping her hair back and turning toward him. She took one step and stopped as he dimmed the light and sat on in a high-back chair. Easing her skirt up, she slowly dipped to the left and then the right, swinging her hips as she let the bass of the saxophone direct the flow of her body.

Bending down in front of him, she whispered in his ear. "Show me the money."

He dug deep into his oversized pants pocket and pulled out at knot of bills.

"Now that's a good, daddy. Poppa, can you make it rain for me?"

"For sure, I can, Momma." Michael started flicking bill after bill into the air as Keisha dipped it low and rolled for his pleasure.

She eased one arm out of her dress and then the other. She bent over him, her breasts slapping him in the face. "You like this, Daddy?"

"Yeah, baby, show me some more."

"Your wish is my command."

Keisha stepped back, grabbed one of her breasts, and brought it up to lick it. Michael pulled out his dick and started stroking it. She slid the dress to her feet, quickly kicked it in the air, and watched it fall. She'd practiced that move routinely after seeing Demi Moore in *Strip Tease* and had been waiting to perform it for someone.

Catching him completely off guard, she lifted her left leg straight up in the air and twirled around, giving him a clear view of her Brazilian wax. She then fell to the floor and bounced up and down.

Michael swallowed hard, his Adam's apple bobbing. "Please come give it me, Momma," he pleaded. His dick was throbbing and he couldn't take any more.

"I don't think you're ready," Keisha said.

"I'm ready. Come on, baby, I need you."

"Scoot to the edge of the chair," she instructed.

When he did, she used her forearms to lift her lower body up as she scooted backwards, raising herself up and settling on top of his thick ten inches. As she rode him like a bulldog, Michael did his best not to cum. He picked her up and started eating her pussy upside down, his delicious-looking dick waving back and forth in her face.

Temptation is a motherfucker, she thought.

He was licking her kitty so good, she felt obligated to return the favor. She grabbed his penis, put it in her mouth, and let the mints assist her in performing her magic.

Michael lifted her up and carried her to the bedroom. Keisha knew that she could be as freaky as she wanted to be with him without worrying about him spreading the word. She told him to put it in her other hole.

"Please be gentle, baby. I'm a virgin there," she lied, nibbling his ear.

It was uncomfortable at first, as she'd known it would be, but, once she loosened up, the pleasure was unbelievable. Dino had gotten her used to that. She tingled with pleasure with his every stroke.

"Girl, I think I just fell in love! You are what I've been looking for all my life," he said, thrusting deeply into her anus.

What a waste of a good dick, she thought after she'd

fucked him to sleep. *He could have* been Sherman's replacement.

Once she was sure he was sleeping deeply, she went to the living room and gathered her things and the money from the floor. It was way more than they'd agreed on. She opened the door for John's boys. Once the masked men were inside, she left.

The next day, she went to see John to get paid.

"Hello, Keisha."

"Hey, John"

"I'm proud of you. You did what it took to get the job done. How did it feel?"

"It felt good. Not at all like I expected."

"Which part?"

"What? Why?" Keisha asked nervously, wondering if he was asking her about the sexual encounter.

"I just want to know."

"It felt good."

"That's all? Just good?" He raised an eyebrow.

"Actually, it felt awesome. But you didn't say that was part of the game."

"It's not. You made that decision."

"You're right, I did. And, I must admit, I enjoyed it." Keisha giggled.

"What did you enjoy the most?"

"I enjoyed knowing that I would be the last female he would ever be with."

John got up from behind his desk and walked over to Keisha. He looked her straight in the eyes and asked, "So you like dominating?"

Keisha turned her head and looked at the floor, blushing, before looking back up at him. "Yes, I guess."

"So, if you fuck me, how would that make you feel?"

Without hesitating, she said, "Like I'm fucking power."

Secretly, she lusted for John. She'd never slept with an older man before, but the sexual experience wasn't what interested her. She was more attracted to the benefits she could get from him. And knowing that she had one of Chicago's most powerful men at her disposal would be an ultimate high.

He pulled her to him and kissed her. "Fuck me like you fucked him, but better."

Keisha leaned against his desk, lifted up her dressed, and spread her legs. She knew that awesome sex was another way to a man's heart and she planned to win him over. She fucked and sucked him until he couldn't get it up anymore.

That day, she became his thrill, not his woman. Every man needs a thrill and a comfort in their life. The thrill is the one who does what the main woman can't or won't do. She goes on all the nice trips, attends the big social parties, and does whatever she wants. Everyone knows the thrill, but they only hear about the wife.

The wife must be protected at all times. Most men claim not to love their thrill. They'll say quickly that she's just a jump-off, someone they have around for freaky fun. But in all honesty, the jump-off is the one he truly craves. He just knows that she'll be hard to tame. From experience, Keisha knew the game all too well.

Chapter 16

After a while, setting up guys didn't faze them. The more they set up, the more money they earned. They no longer needed the money from the streets. Sherrie moved into her own apartment, Tameka and Big Man were still going strong, and Keisha had John to replace Sherman's sexual duties. All three ladies were unapologetic and living life in the fast lane.

They were at their favorite hangout spot in Hyde Park, eating and chitchatting.

Keisha cleared her throat and changed the subject from what they'd been talking about.

"You know who's next on the list, don't you, Tameka?" she asked.

"No and I don't give a fuck. My only concern is the amount of mula I'll get." She high-fived Sherrie.

"I'm glad you feel that way because it's June."

Sherrie dropped her fork in her salad. She looked at Keisha in disbelief.

"June who?" Tameka asked. The words came out in a high pitch and the smile fell from her lips, A frown replaced it, wrinkling her forehead. She looked uncertain and nervous, waiting for Keisha to respond.

"Your ex, June. He owes John over seventy G's."

Tameka sat silent, a look of despair and shock on her face. She didn't know what to think, say, or do. Slowly, she shook her head. In a low voice, she mumbled, "I can't do it, I can't set him up to be … to be …" She couldn't fix her mouth to say murdered. The very thought of June not living brought tears to her eyes.

"Sure you can't, Tameka." Sherrie rubbed Tameka's arm. "We understand that. Don't we, Keisha."

"Yes I do. I totally understand. Don't you worry about it, I'll do it," Keisha reached across the table to pat Tameka's hand, then proceeded to continue eating her food.

At a loss for words, Sherrie just looked at her.

"No, none of us can," Tameka, said raising her voice. She now had a look of disgust on her face. She was baffled by her best friend's eagerness to kill the man she loved and for whom she had birthed a son.

Keisha stopped eating, shocked by Tameka's words. "Why not?"

"Keisha, he's Emonie's daddy."

"No, *Big Man* is Emonie's daddy."

"Listen, we all know the truth about who his daddy is, stop fucking with me."

"So what are you saying?" Keisha said, irritated. She picked up a napkin to wipe her mouth.

"I'll pay his debt."

"Are you fucking crazy? You don't have that type of money to give away. Plus, you know once you make the list, there's no getting off."

"Keisha, you're fucking John."

"So? What does that have to do with it? I can't tell that man how to run his business. Besides, I don't want him to know you're weak for a nigga who doesn't give a fuck about you. Let's just set his ass up and go on with our lives."

"Damn, bitch, Dino really did a job on you. You really don't give a fuck, do you?"

"Hell no, and you shouldn't either."

"Let the truth be told, we're probably part of the reason he's on the list," Tameka said.

"Probably so, and I still don't give a fuck. June didn't care about using you to sell his shit," Keisha reminded her.

"Just like Dino didn't care about using you like a punching bag and fucking your mother," Tameka spat back.

Unable to believe Tameka went there, Keisha jumped up.

The two got in each other's face, ready to go blow for blow. Customers at other tables and at the bar stared at them, trying to figure out what all the commotion was.

Sherrie stepped between them and ordered them to lower their voices.

"Calm down, both of y'all. We're sisters. We're not going to let a nigga come between us. Please take a seat, for God's sake," Sherrie pleaded.

"You know what, Tameka?" Keisha said between clenched teeth. "You're absolutely right. Dino didn't give a fuck about me and neither did my mom. And that's why I don't give a fuck now. People only do to you what you allow them to do. Unlike you, I refuse to allow a bitch-ass nigga or a drug-addicted trick use me again."

Keisha's eyes got teary, anger and hurt in her eyes, as she stared Tameka down. She was so livid she could have snatched the life out of Tameka. Instead, she grabbed her purse and keys off the table, put on her sunglasses, and left.

"Tameka, what the hell is wrong with you?" Sherrie said. "You might not want to hear what I have to say, but you were dead wrong." She couldn't believe what had just taken place.

"Wrong for what? Wanting my child's father to live?"

"No, for what you said to Keisha, throwing Dino and her mother in her face. You know she didn't have any control over that. But you, on the other hand, had control over June using you and getting pregnant. That was foul, Tameka, and you know it."

It was almost two in the morning and Keisha couldn't sleep, her argument with Tameka on her mind. She decided if she had to set June up herself, behind Sherrie and Tameka's backs, she would. There was no way that she was going to let him get in the way of her financial goal.

Her phone rang.

Who the hell is this calling me this late at night?

Looking at the caller ID, she saw that it was one of John's numbers.

"Hello?" she answered, using a fake sleepy voice.

"Hello, Keisha, it's Dave. John sent me over to pick you up."

"Pick me up for what?"

"I don't know, Ma. I don't ask questions, I just do what I'm told."

"Okay, here I come. Let me slip on some clothes. Give me a minute."

Keisha threw on her Juicy Couture sweats, brushed her teeth, took off her hair-scarf, and unwrapped her hair. She headed downstairs to the black Escalade sitting on twenty-six inch chrome spinners that awaited her.

When she got to John's spot, he was standing in the door to greet her.

"Hello, princess. I know it's late, but I need to be in you right now."

You could've came to me, Keisha thought, but she just smiled and said nothing.

"I want to try something with you," John continued.

"What?" a reluctant Keisha asked. "You know I don't do that funny, extra-freaky crap."

"I know, baby," he said, laughing.

"Go take a shower, and when you come out, meet me in the kitchen with nothing on."

All types of thoughts went through Keisha's head while she showered.

If this bastard got a bitch, another dude, or a camera out there, I'm going to die tonight because I will try to kill his ass.

Ten minutes after hearing the shower get turn off, John said, "Come out, princess. What's taking you so long?"

"Here I come."

She entered the room in her birthday suit just as he'd instructed. Looking around, she breathed a sigh of relief when she didn't see a third person or anything out of the ordinary.

John turned and looked at her. "You are amazing," he said.

"Well, thank you, big daddy." She twirled around to give him a full view of her physique. She was proud of the body she worked hard to maintain. She knew that a toned, sexy, shapely body was just as important as a pretty face, if not more. She got off on being a triple threat. She referred to herself as the 3Bs—body, brains, and beauty.

"I want to do something that I've never done before or had the urge to until I met you. Go over to the kitchen counter." John admired her rear as she strolled slowly to the kitchen making sure he got a nice view.

Okay this is strange, she thought. *I know he's had sex on a kitchen countertop before. What the hell is he up to?*

John walked over to Keisha, placed his hand around her small waist, and lifted her up onto the countertop. He kissed her neck, and then her lips passionately as he used a finger to play with her pussy. Keisha was hot and ready to go, but he pulled himself back when she started unfastening his pants.

"No, not yet, baby. I told you I want to try something different. Now lay on your back and spread your legs."

She did everything that she was instructed to.

He went to the refrigerator and got some ice cream, whipped cream, caramel and a jar of cherries. He spread the ice cream between her legs and she jerked a little from the coldness of it. It felt good in an uncomfortable way. He dipped the spoon in the whipped cream and spread it over the ice cream, then squeezed the caramel on top.

"What sundae is complete without a cherry?" he

asked.

After his preparations were done, he took his spoon and started eating his human ice cream sundae. The ice cream was melting and running down between her butt cheeks, causing Keisha to squirm in discomfort. John dove in with his tongue, going for the treasure that was buried beneath the sundae.

"Oh, my God, this feels good. Don't stop," Keisha pleaded.

She lifted up her torso in an attempt to get John to lick her ass, but every time she rose, he pulled her back down.

This must be heaven. I can't believe that the biggest man in the city is eating ice cream off my pussy. He's eating my shit like it's his last meal.

He sucked, licked, pulled, and tongue fucked Keisha until sunrise. She lost track of how many orgasms she had.

Chapter 17

A week after their argument, Keisha and Tameka were sitting at Sherrie's apartment, avoiding looking at each other. The room was so quiet you could hear a stick pin drop. They hadn't spoken to each other since their argument.

Sherrie had called them over to put an end to them not speaking. They have never stopped speaking before and she didn't like it.

The only reason Keisha came was that Sherrie had told her that Tameka wanted to apologize and she wanted to find out what Tameka decided to do about June. Her stomach started growling and her patience was running short. If Sherrie wasn't going to initiate the conversation soon with Tameka, she would. She didn't understand why Tameka was making such a big deal out of this.

Keisha stood and walked by the front door near the TV and looked directly at Tameka. She felt mild sympathy for Tameka as she looked at her, but knew that if they didn't follow through with the job, there wouldn't be any more to come. And that would interfere with her plans. She wasn't going to let that happen. She refused to lose her source of income over her friend loving a dog ass nigga. She loved Tameka like a sister, but she also understood what needed to be done for all their sakes.

She wanted June out the picture. She knew that if he stayed alive, one day he would come to retaliate for what she'd stolen from him. With him gone, she'd have one less person to watch her back from.

"Listen, I'm about to go," she said. "I need to eat, so we need to discuss this business and move on. Tameka, what are you going to do? If you can't handle it, like I said before, I will."

Tameka looked up at Keisha, her face emotionless. Turning her head, she said, "I'll take care of him tonight."

"What do you plan on doing?" Sherrie asked, concerned.

"I'll call him this evening and tell him that I need to talk to him. We'll hook up and I'll slip some of that stuff we got left over that Keisha's cousin gave us in his drink, then let John's boys in to do the rest."

"Are you sure you can handle that?" Keisha asked with a skeptical look.

"Yes, I can. June doesn't know anything about what we do. He'd never suspect me of trying to set him up."

Keisha crossed her arms. "We need to get this shit over and done with."

Tameka glared at her. "You're so damn anxious to kill my baby's daddy."

"Are we going to go there again, Tameka?" Keisha asked.

"No, we are not," Sherrie piped in. "Listen, we have all been friends way too long to let anything come between us, especially a guy. Y'all have to stop this shit. We knew when we signed up for this that maybe we'd have to set up someone we know. Plus it's too late to pull out. So let's get this over with, and go back to us being us. I don't want to have to set up Emonie's biological father either, Tameka, but we have to do what we have to do. Plus, Emonie doesn't know him and you're no longer with him. With that being said, I do understand your reasons and respect your feelings."

"That's true," Keisha said. I love y'all and I know sometimes I come across as a bitch with no emotions, but in this world, you have to be a bitch to get money, power, and respect. I don't want y'all to ever experience the torment that I endured from fucking with a guy who doesn't give a rat's ass about you and a mother who looks at you just as a source of income. We can't let a man come between us, we're blood sisters. I still have the cut on my finger to prove it. We need to take care of this and whatever else we need to until we have enough money to move our families out the hood," She looked at Tameka. "Are you absolutely sure you can carry this out?"

"Yeah, I got this. Don't worry. I'll call y'all once everything is done."

Keisha had a gut feeling that Tameka wasn't strong enough to follow the order through and wanted badly to persuade her into letting her take care of June. Instead, she went with the flow and kept her thoughts to herself. "A'ight, I'm out. I'll talk to you ladies later. I'm going to go eat.

Keisha stopped to check the time again. The time was 3:36 a.m. and there was still no word from Tameka yet. She paced her floor, holding her cell phone tight in her hand. Her mind wouldn't allow her to rest. She worried about her friends and that she may have put her life in danger for money.

Her phone vibrated, she answered immediately. "Tameka?"

No, it's Sherrie. So I take it that you haven't heard from her either?

"No, I thought that you were her. I see you can't sleep either."

"Girl, I've been up all day. My body tired, but my mind isn't.

"I know the feeling."

"I'm sitting her watching reruns of *Good Times* and eating butter pecan ice cream."

"Sherrie, you know better than to eat all that sugar after seven."

"I know, right? A bitch gonna get fat. I'll never get a husband then."

They start laughing.

"Girl, if a man can't look past a couple of extra pounds, then you don't need him."

"Yeah, whatever. Would you date a chunky guy?"

"Hell to the no."

"That's so hypocritical for you to say then."

"I know, but you know I'm a vain person. It's nothing new."

"Whatever happened to that guy at your graduation?"

"Nothing much."

"He was fine."

"Yes, he was and he had skills."

"What?" Sherrie almost choked on the spoonful of ice cream she'd just put in her mouth.

"You heard me."

"You slept with him?"

"Yep, a few times."

"When?"

"When I first moved here. He was the first guy to make me ever experience an orgasm.

"What? You been fucking for how long and never experienced one?

"That's right. So, until him, I guess I was an orgasm virgin."

"Why didn't you tell us you were sexing him?"

I wanted to keep it on the low. Plus, I didn't need the pressure of y'all telling me that he was good for me."

"What happened? Do y'all still talk?"

"No. He wanted something serious and I just wanted his sex."

"Keisha, you can't let Dino scare you from men emotionally. All men aren't like him. I've never been in a sexual relationship before, but I have aunts and uncles that have been married for decades and they act like they just met. Dude seemed like a nice guy. You should have given him a chance."

"See, that's exactly why I didn't tell y'all. Have you tried calling Tameka?"

"Yeah, she didn't answer. I called her before I called you."

"Maybe she at home sleep. I know this was hard on her. We just have to wait to hear from her. I may as well lay down. I'll call you later.

"Yeah, me too. Aight"

The next morning, the light from the sun beamed into Keisha's condo and onto her face. Too lazy to get up and pull the drapes closed, she pulled a throw blanket over her face to block the light. Her cell phone started vibrating. She searched the sofa frantically for it, thinking it might be Tameka. It stopped vibrating, but started again.

Where is this damn phone? Maybe they'll leave a message, she thought.

The caller was determined to talk to Keisha. The phone vibrated back to back, non-stop. She finally found it buried deep between the wood and cushion of the sofa.

She looked at her phone and saw that it was John. She exhaled loudly.

"Hello?" she answered, sounding groggy.

"You and your girls need to get my office now," John ordered and hung up.

What the hell is going on? I bet it has something to do with June's ass. I knew I should have set him up myself.

Keisha immediately called Tameka. When there was no answer on her cell phone, she called her house phone. *Please pick up.*

"Hello," A perky Tameka answered. Keisha was relieved to hear her voice.

"Why didn't you call me and let me know how everything went? What happened last night?"

"Nothing," Tameka whispered into the phone.

"What do you mean, nothing?"

"What I said. Exactly nothing," Tameka said in a snappy voice. She was fed up with Keisha thinking that she ran shit.

Tameka walked out of the kitchen where her, Big

Man, and Emonie were eating breakfast. She didn't want Big Man to hear her conversation.

"Bitch, can you elaborate?" Keisha snapped back.

"I didn't go through with it last night because the timing wasn't right."

"Timing?"

"Yeah, timing. He was acting suspicious. I didn't know if he told someone that he was meeting me or not. I'll do it another day."

"Another day? What the hell do you think this is, Tameka, a game? It's not that simple. John wants what he wants *when* he want it. We work for him. We follow his instructions, not set our own. We have to meet him at his office right now. Can you make it or do you need to reschedule?" Keisha asked sarcastically.

"I'll be there!" Tameka said before hanging the phone up on Keisha

"No that heifer didn't," Keisha said out loud, looking at her phone. "Silly bitch got some nerves."

Keisha sat in front of John's office waiting for Tameka and Sherrie to pull up. She spotted Sherrie, flagged her down, and filled her in on the situation. An hour later, Tameka drove up. Keisha and Sherrie stared at her with upset and disappointed looks on their faces. John's armed security escorted them to his office. It was a big empty warehouse with a huge executive desk and a three chairs sitting in the middle.

"This is a bit much, don't you think?" Sherrie said in a low voice, leaning over to Keisha.

Keisha nodded.

"Hello, ladies. Take a seat," John said from behind his desk.

"Hello, John," they all said nervously. They took a seat in the three chairs that was spaced apart from each other in front of the desk. John walked around each of their chairs, making eye contact with them, then sat on the armrest of Tameka's chair.

Her heart started to beat fast.

Sherrie and Keisha gave each other wide-eyed look and then looked at a clearly nervous and uncomfortable Tameka.

"Tameka, what happened last night? My guys were there and they said you never opened the door."

Tameka took a deep breath and adjusted herself in the chair. "John, the time wasn't right. He was actin' like he thought something was up and he was strapped. I didn't want to take a chance on me or one of your guys or myself getting injured or killed."

"Bullshit!" John screamed, bending down in her face.

They all jumped in their chairs. They'd never heard John raise his voice before. He was normally a soft-spoken person. Never had they seen this side of him. He was really pissed. The vein in his temple was popping.

"John, it's the truth." Tameka said.

"Tameka, don't give me that shit. You think I don't know that you used to fuck that clown? I know everything. I'm like God around this here. It's not one thing that goes down in these streets that I don't know about. Seriously, are you going to let something as little as feelings stop you from making money? You can't have emotions with this job; I told you that. You lucky that you're Andre peoples, other then that I'll killed you right here. Instead I'm going to give you time to think about what important to you, his life or yours."

Keisha knew that if Tameka didn't stand up now and say hers' was more important to her, her ass would be on the list next. They knew too much for him to just let them out without them proving their loyalty and fear of him. Tameka's not getting the job done last night proved that she wasn't scared of the consequences from him. Although she was furious with Tameka, she wouldn't to let him harm her. She knew Sherrie felt the same way. They all would end up on the list before they let him kill her.

"I'll set him up again tonight for half the pay." Tameka's voice shook.

John stood up. "That's what I want to hear. Ladies, you may leave. Keisha, you stay."

Tameka and Sherrie shot Keisha a look. Sherrie shook her head discreetly, telling Keisha no, not to stay. She was unsure of Keisha's safety and didn't trust leaving her with John.

"I'll catch up with y'all later," Keisha said. She figured he wanted to fuck. But she had no intention of fulfilling his desire after he'd just threatened to take her best friend's life,.

"Are you sure?" Sherrie said with a concerned looked..

"Yeah, I'm cool." Keisha leaned back in the chair and crossed her legs. looking up at John.

Sherrie watched Keisha to see if she was scared. Still unsure, she turned and left with Tameka.

John's face and voice were back to normal—calm and collected "I got you something."

"What?"

"Close your eyes." He walked behind his desk, picked up a big box from the floor, and set it on the desk.

Keisha wasn't scared that John was going to do any bodily harm to her. She closed her eyes.

She felt something heavy on her back.

"Open your eyes."

She opened her eyes and rubbed her hand down the silky, Black Diamond mink that he'd draped over her shoulders.

"This is for me?" she asked, grinning.

"Yeah, baby, you deserve it. Nothing but the best for my princess."

Keisha had tons of furs before, but not a Black Diamond. Feeling that a simple thank you wasn't enough, she pushed him down in the chair and got on her knees. She unzipped his pants and took his manhood into her mouth, using all the skills she'd learned over the years and took him to a place that she knew no other woman had taken him.

Returning back to the world, he opened his eyes and looked down at her, placing his penis back into his boxers.

"You are so beautiful and amazing to me. I've never in my life met a woman like you. I want you to stop working and be my lady."

Her mouth still full of his nut, she almost choked.

John smiled. "I know it's a lot to swallow."

Keisha shot him a mean look and got up to spit in the wastebasket. "Funny, ha-ha, I see you got jokes."

"What, baby? I'm just saying."

"Yeah, nice choice of words, funny man. I'm glad to see you got your sense of humor back." She took a deep breath. "You want me to be your what? What about your wife?"

He shrugged. "What about her?"

"Where's she going?"

"Nowhere."

Keisha shook her head and turned away from him. "I'm sorry, John, but I can't be number two."

"What do you mean, princess? You're already number two. You've just got more leeway than her. Think about it for a day or two; you don't have to answer now." He grabbed her by the waist from behind and pulled her body into his. "Baby, just think about it."

Keisha nodded and left.

On the drive home, she thought about it. *I can't be his girl. I'm his thrill, not the bitch stuck in the house wondering where he is or who he's with. Then again, I have been number two. If I say yeah, it'll mean more money to shop with and driving the latest luxury car. Hell, I could even use his money to open my marketing company.*

She got excited thinking about all the material things she would gain by becoming his woman. Then she quickly came back to reality. *Who am I fooling? Once I get that title, it'll be a wrap. Another bitch will replace me. But if I say no, what'll happen to our business arrangement?*

That night, Keisha and Sherrie made sure Tameka did what she had to do. They drove her to meet June themselves and waited outside for three hours until she got up to let John's boys in and returned to the car.

"Are you okay, Tameka?" Sherrie asked.

"Yeah, I'm okay. That bastard deserves everything he's going to get."

"Why the change of heart?" Keisha said, looking at Tameka through her rearview mirror.

"Not once did that bastard ask me about how I've been, yesterday or today. Instead, he was talkin' about how he's fucked up money-wise and need me to help him get back on his feet."

Sherrie frowned. "Get the fuck outta here."

"Dude is like the scum of the earth. He lives off bitches," Keisha said.

"Well, he's not going to live off *this* bitch no more." Tameka turned her head and looked out the window

Keisha felt sorry for her "Let's have a pajama party at my place tonight. It'll be like old times. I'll even make your favorite dish, Tameka—banana pudding. From scratch."

"I'm down with that," Sherrie said.

Tameka sighed. "Me too. I need a rest from Emonie and Big Man. I don't know which one is worse, Big Man cry just as much as the damn baby. He can't do shit for himself. Now I see why his last girl left his ass. He thinks he's George Jefferson and I'm his maid, Florence."

Keisha nodded her head. "Yeah, that's how most guys are—lazy, trifling, and selfish-ass bastards,"

"Damn, if I didn't know any better, Keisha, I'd assume that you were a lesbian." Sherrie said.

"Assume your ass. The truth is the truth."

Chapter 18

"**D**amn, we've been in the house all day," Sherrie said, stretching.

Tameka plopped down on Keisha's couch next to her. "Yeah, I don't know when was the last time I did this"

"Hell, living with Dino's ass, I did it often. That Negro was so insecure of another guy swooping me up, he didn't want me to go out to the mailbox. My only outing was school. That's why I took so many damn classes."

"I still can't believe that you set his ass up," Sherrie said.

Keisha looked at her. "Hell, y'all just don't know how many times I plotted how I was gonna escape from his ass without being empty-handed. Living with him was a fucking nightmare."

"I guess the luxury gifts were the dream," Tameka said.

"Cash rules everything around me, cream get that money dolla, dolla after muthafucking bill, y'all!" Keisha sang the chorus of *C.R.E.A.M.* with her own added twist.

They all chuckled.

She got up to pour them drinks. "Seriously, y'all know that I used to love Dino. The money was only part of it. After years of verbal and physical abuse, the love was gone. But I used to be so much in love with that man his shit smelled like flowers to me."

Sherrie grimaced. "Damn, now that's love!"

"I felt that way about June," Tameka said. "I know we weren't together as long as you and Dino, but love don't have a time frame. At times, he made me feel like I was the only person that existed in the world. He'd give me a look that made my heart skip a beat. I don't know what happened between us that made him change."

Keisha walked over to the sofa and handed them each a glass of champagne before sitting down and propping her legs up on the glass sofa table.

"Tameka, the love of money is the root of all evil," she said. "It makes you do some strange things. Trust me, I know. Men know that money gives you power and a man that needs to use a woman to get that money will make her feel weak emotionally. We women are emotional creatures. Hell, Dino use to fuck me over, physically, mentally, and emotionally, making me doubt myself. He tried his damnedest to fuck my body up with a baby. Can you imagine a little Dino walking around here? Yes, he would be a handsome little boy, but, damn, he probably would've been just as fucked up as his daddy when he got older. I was the only family that man had and he treated me like I wasn't even human."

Sherrie was quiet, listening to Tameka and Keisha. She felt sorry for them. They'd endured so much pain from their mothers, fathers, and men in general. Her only pain was the fact that her interaction with her own father so far had been prison visits. But, even with that, she was still in a better situation than they were. She knew her father and he was still alive and her mother wasn't a drunk or a drug addict. She really didn't have a reason to be on the streets hustling. She did it just to fit in.

"Okay, snap out of it before y'all asses get depressed." She tried to change the mood. "Let's hit the club. We haven't been out in a while. I have some new moves that I saw in a video that I want to try out."

Keisha sipped from her glass. "Cool, I'm down with that. I feel like stunting on some bitches tonight anyway. I bought a pair of bad-ass multi-snake pumps from Nordstrom the other day."

"Fuck it," Tameka said. "Count me in. I can't get in any more trouble than I'm in with Big Man already. I know he been blowin' my phone up. I told him I needed some air."

They raided Keisha's closet. Keisha put on a white, three-quarter sleeve leather mini dress. Although it was winter, after Labor Day, and snowy outside, she didn't care. Her plan was to stand out. Besides that, her Black Diamond full-length mink would keep her warm.

Sherrie put on one of Keisha's bodysuits with cutouts on the side and Tameka kept it simple, choosing a satin blouse, jeans, and riding boots.

Sherrie looked at her watch. "Come on y'all. It's getting late. I at least need two hours of shaking my ass and grinding on some lucky fool on the dance floor."

After putting the finishing touches on hair and make-up, they finally left. They were headed to Chicago's number one club on a Sunday, The Clique. They knew every baller in the Chi would be there. The line of people trying to get in was always wrapped around the corner. The only ones able to get in front of the line had paper, hung tight with the muthafucka with the paper, or was a girl who fucked the bouncers.

They were picky about who they let in. You either had to be beautiful, sexy, or have a bad-ass shape with an apple bottom. Lucky for Tameka, Keisha, and Sherrie, they had it all. They walked straight to the front of the line and right past security. They could hear the music thumping from outside, the bass sending a vibration through their bodies.

Sherrie bobbed her head to the beat, anxious to hit the dance floor. "That's my song," she said. "I'll meet y'all at the bar later. I'm on the floor."

"Hey Keisha, there go Pat and 'nem from the block. I'm 'bout to go holla at them," Tameka said.

"A'ight."

Keisha wasn't much of a dancer and she really didn't mess with the neighborhood guys like Tameka and Sherrie did. She walked over to the bar and ordered a drink. Chilling, she got lost in her thoughts, trying to figure out how she was going to tell John that she wasn't digging him like that and wondering what the outcome would be.

Looking up to tell the bartender to pour her another drink, she saw an older guy walk behind her in the mirror. *I know that's not who I think that is,* she thought. She turned slightly for a better look. *Yes, the hell it is.*

It was Jeff, one of her mother's ex-boyfriends. *What the fuck is his old ass doing up in here? And wearing that old-ass velour Jordan jogging suit. This bitch told me I was going to grow up to be a drug addict and a loser like my mom. Let me walk my fine ass past him. I can't wait to see his reaction when he sees me.*

Getting up from her stool, she strolled past him.

"Hey, lady," he said. "You just gon' walk right past me?"

Keisha looked him up and down. "Excuse me, do I know you?"

"Quit playing, girl. It's me, Jeff."

"Jeff?" She pretended not to know who he was. "Oh, Jeff. Damn, you look different."

"You look good, girl!"

"I know. So what you been up to? Are you still robbing the cradle and belittling females to feel more like a man?"

He laughed. "I never belittle a woman and I no longer fuck with gold-digging little bitches. I realized that I'm not Captain Save-a-hoe, I can't bed self-proclaimed reformed addicts who steal your money and products, or turn a whore into a housewife."

Keisha put her hands on her hips and narrowed her eyes. "What the hell do you mean by that?"

"I gave your mom everything she craved, not just what she needed, and she left me heartbroken and damn near broke."

"Did you forget that you left my mother and me in a house to get evicted in the middle of December while you took some young bitch to the Bahamas? No hard feelings, though," she said sarcastically.

"Well, I guess you got your mother's talent of getting a nigga to take care of you. You look spiffy."

"Thank you. I take care of myself."

"Cool, why don't you buy me a drink since you got it like that, Miss Independent?"

"Negro, please. The only person I spend my money

on is *me*. Besides, if you can't afford to buy yourself a drink, you shouldn't be drinking."

"Damn, you're coldhearted. A nigga not good for a drink?"

"I'll holla. Deuces." She threw up a peace sign, turning it into a fuck you and walked away.

That bum is a loser on so many levels, she thought. *Damn, that made my day.* She heard a ruckus near the dance floor. *Damn, black people can't party without fighting? Only in the fucking ghetto. Every time some loser gets liquor in their system, a damn fight breaks out.*

The DJ turned off the music and she heard Sherrie's voice. Keisha dropped her drink and quickly maneuvered her way through the crowd to the dance floor. Getting closer, she spotted Sherrie and a chick who looked like the one in the car with June the day they'd beat him down.

"Bitch, yeah it's me, so what the fuck is you gon' do?" Sherrie said.

"Bitch, you got some nerves to be talking shit now."

The girl and her friends crowded around Sherrie. Keisha pushed her way through the crowd, not taking her eyes off Sherrie. When she finally made her way to the stage, Tameka appeared from nowhere, hitting the chick on the head with a chair.

Sherrie stole off the other girl and Keisha came from behind and put another girl in a headlock, punching her in the face and kicking another girl that the crowd had pushed to the floor.

Keisha kicked off her pumps and she and Tameka resumed throwing blows, knocking bitches out. Security came through and started picking up people and tossing them out the door. Two of the security guards who knew them from the hood grabbed the two girls and told Keisha and Tameka to leave before the cops came.

"Where the hell is Sherrie, Tameka?" Keisha looked around, stretching to look around the crowd. "I don't see her."

A girl from around the way handed Keisha her shoes and told them Sherrie was out back, fighting in the alley. They ran out back where five girls were kicking and stomping Sherrie, who lay helpless on the ground. Tameka pulled out her piece and let one go in the air. The group scattered, leaving Sherrie's battered body lying in the bloodstained snow.

Tameka looked down at her friend and tears filled her eyes. "Fuck no, these bitches is about to pay." She took off running after the girls.

"Somebody call the paramedics, please," Keisha yelled, pleading with onlookers. Tears ran down her face, leaving tracks from her makeup, as she leaned over Sherrie. "You're going to be okay. Hang in there, sister, I got you."

"I'm cold," Sherrie mumbled, trembling and coughing up blood.

"I know, honey, we all are. We're in the windy city, you know." Keisha tried to joke and not look too worried so she wouldn't upset Sherrie.

One of the bouncers brought Keisha her coat. Taking it, she covered Sherrie with it to keep her warm.

She picked up Sherrie's hands and held them. "I got you. Don't worry."

A loud shot went off somewhere down the street.

Oh, God, Keisha thought. *Where the fuck is Tameka?*

Pat, one of their friends from the neighborhood, pulled up in his truck. "Come on. We'll take her to the hospital. These muthafuckas are taking too long to come."

They lifted Sherrie and placed her in the back seat of his Range Rover, her blood staining the cream-colored leather seat.

Keisha looked around impatiently to see if she could see Tameka, but her friend was nowhere in sight. She didn't want to leave her, but she knew she had to get Sherrie to the emergency room ASAP. Her instincts told her that the gunshot she heard hadn't hit Tameka.

Keisha sat in a chair in the hospital waiting room, rocking back in forth, waiting for Sherrie to come out of surgery. Seeing Tameka walk in, she let out a deep breath and rushed to her, hugging her tight.

"Where in the hell have you been? I've been blowing your phone up."

Tameka ignored the question. "How is she?"

"I don't know. She's still in surgery. Nobody has come out yet to tell me shit. Where were you?"

"I had to handle something," Tameka's voice was shrill and she had a funny look on her face.

Looking at her, Keisha knew exactly what had happened. Tameka had the same look Keisha had the night she'd killed Reggie. It was a combination of fear, confusion, doubt, nervousness, happiness, pride, grief and power.

A nurse finally came from behind the two steel double doors and called for the family of Sherrie James. Keisha and Tameka rushed up to her.

"Are you the family of Sherrie James?" she asked them.

"Yes, we're her sisters," Keisha said.

"The surgery was a success. The doctor will be out to talk to you very soon."

"Thank you, ma'am." Tameka's legs got weak and she sank to the floor. And thank you, God."

Keisha covered her face with her hands, crying tears of joy and relief.

A few minutes later, the doctor walked out and removed his surgical mask. "Are you both the patient's relatives?" he asked.

"Yes, doctor. They're her sisters," the nurse told him.

"How is she doing, Doctor?" Keisha asked.

"Young lady, your sister is lucky to be alive. The knife missed a main artery by a half inch."

"Thank you doctor, for everything." Tameka said.

They listened as the doctor explained Sherrie's injuries and the care she would need for the next few months.

From the corner of her eye, Keisha noticed the triage nurse talking to two men with badges on their jackets and guns on their hips. The nurse pointed in their direction and the men walked toward them.

She elbowed Tameka to get her attention. Tameka looked up and followed Keisha eyes. When she saw the men heading towards them, a jolt of fear shot through her and her stomach flipped.

"Excuse me, Doctor." The six-foot-tall, muscular, bald, white detective interrupted the doctor, showing his badge. "My name is Detective Fitzgerald and this is my partner Detective Smith." He gestured to the other officer, a short, stocky, black man. "We need to talk to these two ladies."

The doctor nodded and walked to the nurse's desk a few feet away.

The detective turned his blue-eyed gaze to Keisha and Tameka. "I understand that you were involved in a brawl tonight at a club called The Clique that ended up with a girl being shot dead."

Keisha looked directly at him. "Detective, we're sorry to hear that about someone dying, but we're suffering here too. Our sister almost lost her life. I'm not sure how we could be of any assistance to you, sir. We had nothing to do with anything. All we know is that our sister went on the dance floor to dance and then we heard her scream. She got jumped and stabbed. Maybe the person who stabbed her is the same person who shot the girl."

"Is that your statement?" Detective Smith asked.

"No, Detective, it's not a statement. I'm just telling you what I know," Keisha used her best innocent voice.

He turned and looked at Tameka. She fidgeted under his stare, unable to look him in the eyes. He knew in his gut that they had something to do with the murder, but without evidence, he couldn't prove it or do anything about it.

"What about your sister? Maybe she saw something that could help us.

The doctor rejoined the group and shook his head. "I'm sorry, Detective. I'm her doctor and she's not stable enough to answer any questions tonight. You'll have to come back tomorrow."

Detective Fitzgerald sighed. "Okay, Doctor. We'll come back tomorrow. As for you ladies, stick around in case we have more questions."

Detective Smith looked directly at Tameka. "We'll

definitely see you ladies around."

Tameka looked away, his stare sending a chill through her body.

After the detectives left, Keisha turned to the doctor. "Will we be able to see her tonight?"

The doctor shook his head. "I'm sorry, but no visitors tonight. If you'll excuse me, I have to go now."

Keisha watched him walk down the hall before turning to a distraught Tameka. "Damn, Tameka, we gotta clear this shit up."

"I know!" Tameka said pacing back and forth with her hands on her head.

"Were you careful?"

"Yes." She didn't go into detail.

"Where's the piece?"

"I got rid of it."

"Are you sure? Where nobody can find it?"

"Lake Michigan."

"Good, you did clean your prints off, right?"

"Yes!" Tameka snapped. She stopped pacing and faced Keisha. "Damn, you acting like the fucking dicks now. What the fuck?" She took a deep breath and closed her eyes, holding back tears. "That bitch deserved what she got. She should've known better than to fuck with us. I had to handle her; she tried to kill our sista."

To Keisha, it sounded as if Tameka was reassuring herself about what she'd done. She pulled her into a hug. "You're absolutely right. May she live eternally in hell." She stepped back and looked at Tameka. "We can't see Sherrie tonight, so let's go. I'm tired. This has been a long, stressful night. No more clubs for me."

Tameka nodded and turned to follow her, wiping her eyes. "Me either. I need to go hug my son and smoke a blunt to calm my nerves before calling Sherrie's mom."

"Oh, yes, you do. I'm so glad you volunteered to call her, because I sure don't want to. I can't deal with her blaming us for what happened. I can hear her now. 'What did y'all do to my baby?'"

"She's not going to say that."

Keisha stopped walking and raised an eyebrow. "When have we not gotten the blame for anything that happened to Sherrie? You know she can't stand her baby girl hanging with us."

Tameka frowned. "Yeah, I guess you have a point." She sighed and started walking again, heading for the exit.

"Oh, wait a minute, Tameka," Keisha said. "I have to get my coat."

Turning back around, she went back to the nurse's station and asked for Sherrie's personal property. The nurse went into the room and came back out with a bag of clothes.

"There should have also been a fur coat," Keisha said.

"Oh, let me check again."

The nurse went back into the room and came back with a much larger bag. Keisha took the bag with the coat in it and smiled at her before going back to where Tameka waited for her.

"Those detectives will not be giving this to one of their wives, talking about keeping it for evidence. Not my Black Diamond."

"I don't blame you. They sure would've if the nurses didn't beat 'em to it."

A week went by and Sherrie was still in the hospital. Tameka and Keisha had visited daily. Still afraid to face her mother, they'd timed their arrivals to avoid running into her. Neither admitted it out loud, but they felt guilty for not being there to prevent Sherrie from getting stabbed.

"Good morning, sunshine," Keisha said, bending over and kissing Sherrie's forehead.

Sherry looked at the clock on the wall. "Good morning to y'all. What the hell are y'all doing up and out this early?" She gave them a knowing look. "Y'all still dodging my mom?"

"Girl, you know your mother is gonna blame us," Tameka said. "She blames us for everything that happens to you."

"That's not true." Sherrie winced as she shifted in the bed.

"What?" Keisha put her hands on her hip. "Sherrie, you know it is. Like when you fell off the merry-go-round and your tooth came out, She said we were spinning you too fast."

"Hell, y'all was." Sherrie tried to smile.

"But, the dentist said that your tooth was coming out anyway. It was already loose. We just sped up the process."

The three of them laughed and Tameka and Keisha squeezed into the twin-sized bed next to Sherrie, being careful not to bump her.

Tameka hugged Sherrie. "All jokes aside, I'm glad that you're okay. I couldn't survive life without you by my side every step of the way."

"Oh, that's so sweet," Sherrie cooed. She continued

dryly, "Too bad a bitch has to get a war wound before she's told how much she's loved by y'all hoes."

"Don't even try it, we tell each other that often," Keisha said.

Sherrie chuckled and lay back on her pillow. "I know. I'm just messing with y'all. I got to get out of this place. My momma, yo momma, Tameka, and friends from church been up here praying for me all day, every day. I finally talked her into going home to get some rest at night." She frowned. "I've seen the news. Somebody got killed the night I got stabbed. Why didn't y'all tell me?"

"Sherrie calm down," Keisha said. "You shouldn't be watching the news, it's depressing. We didn't feel the need to tell you because it's nothing to talk about."

Sherrie looked skeptical. "Some cops came up here last night questioning me. I told them I wasn't conscious, so how in the world would I know what happened? Is there anything I should be concerned about?"

"We got everything covered," Tameka assured her.

"Good. We don't need any murders over our heads."

Keisha and Tameka glanced at each other. They didn't feel the need to tell her what really went down, so they didn't say anything.

Tameka changed the subject. "So when do you go home?"

Sherrie sighed. "I want to go home today, but the doctor said I'll be here until next week," She turned to Keisha. "So, what did you decide to do about John?"

Keisha shrugged. "I haven't decided yet. Hell, I saved enough money to go legit if he decides to cut us off. Y'all did save, right?

"Yeah, I'm straight," Sherrie said. "I even made a

couple of small investments. I'm tired of this lifestyle anyway. This stabbing was an eye opener for me."

"Yeah, me too," Tameka admitted. "I think I'm just going to play the role of a housewife and leave the street shit to Big Man. I'm ready to be a real family."

"Are you sure you don't like John?" Sherrie asked Keisha.

"Trust me, I'm positive. Don't get me wrong. I like John, but not like that. To be honest, I really don't think I'm capable of loving a man again."

"Keisha, don't to let what happened with Dino stop you from letting true love and happiness into your life. All men are *not* the same. There are some good ones out there, I keep telling y'all that."

"Well, where are they?" Tameka asked.

"For real, when you find them, let us know," Keisha said, high-fiving Tameka.

"Big Man is a good guy. He treats you good, Tameka. And, Keisha, don't forget about Sherman. You said he was nice to you."

"Who's Sherman?" Tameka asked. "Oh, is that the fine-ass guy from your school?"

"Yes, he is," Keisha said, giving Sherrie a you-talk-too-much look.

Tameka raised her eyebrows. "Okay, what did I miss? When did you and Sherman hook up?"

"It's nothing, Tameka, trust me. We hooked up a few times and that was it." Keisha explained.

"Nothing? It had to be something enough for you to keep it a secret."

Before Keisha could respond, the nurse walked in and

told them that the morning visiting hours were over, so they had to leave, but they were welcome to come back later.

"Sherrie, we'll see you tomorrow," Tameka said, sliding out of the bed. "Keisha, come on, let's go so you can fill me in on what happened with you and Mister GQ."

Keisha leaned over to kiss Sherrie on the cheek. "You never have been able to keep a secret big mouth," she whispered.

Sherrie smiled and said, "Sorry."

Chapter 19

*T*ameka and Big Man threw a party at their house for Emonie's first birthday.
Sherrie and Tameka's mothers—Jennifer and Mary—hooked up the food and the whole neighborhood came over to celebrate. The two had started hanging out again after Sherrie's stabbing. Jennifer had joined AA and become a member of Mary's church.

Everybody was chilling, playing cards, shooting dice, or doing the electric slide. It was the first party in the hood anyone could remember, where not one fight or argument occurred. Everyone was simply enjoying each other's company.

In the five months since the stabbing, Sherrie had fully recovered and was back to her old self.

"I can't eat any more," she said, leaning back in her chair and unfastening her shorts.

"Here come Big Man and Emonie dressed alike," Keisha said. "I swear that's the only thing that makes Big Man smile—his son." She watched the two interact, admiring their relationship. It reminded her of the relationship she'd had with her dad.

"It's time for my grandbaby to cut his cake," Jennifer said.

Everyone gathered around the table to sing "Happy Birthday." The birthday boy sat in his dad's lap while they sang, looking around at everyone.

When they finished singing, Keisha felt someone staring at her. She looked up and couldn't believe her eyes. She tapped Sherrie, whose mouth dropped open, and she elbowed Tameka. Tameka looked up and dropped the knife she was holding.

"Are you happy to see me or just shocked?" June asked. "You know I wouldn't miss this day."

Tameka stood frozen, her mouth open and her eyes wide.

"Who the fuck are you?" Big Man asked.

June look at Big Man and smirked before walking off.

Tameka's mother took over passing out the cake and Keisha, Tameka, and Sherrie went after him.

They searched the neighborhood but couldn't find him. June seemed to have vanished.

Big Man followed them, questioning Tameka. "Who the fuck was that nigga and what was that all about? Tameka, don't make me kill a muthafucka on my son's birthday. I ain't tryin' to catch a case. You better tell me who that nigga was," he demanded.

"I'll explain everything later," Tameka said, hoping he'd drop it for now." Let's just get back to the party."

After the party, when everybody had left, Tameka told Big Man that June was just a dude that Keisha had some dealings with on the block. She convinced him there was nothing for him to be concerned about and to stay inside with Emonie.

Going back outside, she sat down with Keisha and Sherrie and went over what happened the night she'd set June up. She told them that she had thought he was dead, that she'd left him in in bed asleep and let the guys in to finish him off.

"Maybe they didn't do their part," she said.

Keisha had her doubts. She knew John's boys were soldiers and couldn't imagine them putting him in danger, much less endangering their own by not following his orders. Most of them looked up to him as a father and he treated them well. Keisha couldn't see them biting the hand that fed them. There was no way any of them would slack on the job.

She stood in front of Tameka with her arms folded, looking down at her. "Tameka, be straight with us, did you set him up or was it just a cover-up to get him off the list?"

Tameka jumped up from her chair, tears running down her face. "I swear to you, I did the same thing that we always do." She turned to Sherrie. "You believe me don't you? Sherrie, you know that I would never put y'all in danger, don't you?"

It hurt Sherrie to see Tameka so shaken. We believe you," she said, getting up and hugging her.

Keisha remained silent. She knew firsthand how far a person would go to protect someone they love.

"Keisha?" Tameka's eyes begged her to believe her story.

Keisha paused still unsure. "Yeah, I believe you."

"What about when John finds out?" Tameka said, biting her fingernails. "How will we explain it to him? He won't believe his boys didn't do their job. He'll put me on the list. And he'll think y'all were in on it and put y'all on it too."

"We have to find June and kill him before word gets back to John," Keisha said. "Tameka, do you have any idea where he could be?"

"No, but we can check all his old spots."

Keisha grabbed her keys. "Let's roll."

They went to every spot Tameka could think of, searching into the wee hours of the morning, finding no trace of June. Finally, they headed back to the South Side, deciding to call it a night.

"I'll holla at y'all later," Tameka said, getting out of the car when they pulled up to her house.

"A'ight," Keisha and Sherrie responded. They waited to make sure she got in the house safely before pulling off.

Keisha hit the steering wheel with one hand. "Sherrie, I tell you, it's something about this shit that's not right. I don't trust her right now. I love Tameka, but I just got a funny feeling that she knew that nigga was alive."

Sherrie twisted in her seat to face Keisha. "I do too, Keisha, although I hate to think that she would put us in jeopardy for a man, but I know how much she loves him. What you think we should do?"

"I have not a clue. But I refuse to let John kill any of us, even though, right now, I want to kill her ass my damn self."

"I know, right! That's exactly what John's gonna to do once he finds out June isn't dead."

Keisha pulled onto Sherrie's block and parked in front of her building. She turned towards Sherrie and arched an eyebrow.

"Listen, June knows who put the hit out on him. He probably knows that one of us stole his stash and that we're part of the reason he's on the list. Right now, he's our worry. We'll deal with John later. We have to handle one thing at a time and be cautious with every move."

"True dat," Sherrie said. "My momma always told me to expect the unexpected. She said trust everyone to a certain degree and that your worst enemy can be the one that you trust, love, and honor the most. Keisha, I love Tameka and would do anything for her. But, If she's guilty of faking June's death, then that means she treasures his life more then ours and her own."

Keisha shook her head. "I can't fathom this shit right now. I have to go."

"Me either, Keisha. Me either." Sherrie got out of the car and leaned back in. "Go home and get some rest. We're going to need all our energy to find June before John finds out."

"You're right about that."

"I'll call you later, around noon. Be careful, you know June wants retaliation."

"Yeah, Sherrie, I know. And that's exactly what he'll get," Keisha said, lifting her .45 automatic out of her lap. I love you, Sherrie. I'll see you later.

After watching Sherrie go inside, she sped off.

Keisha, Tameka, and Sherrie drove around for days—morning, noon, and night—but found no sign of June. Keisha and Sherrie grew more and more suspicious of Tameka.

"Sherrie pull this bitch over," a frustrated Keisha demanded. "Tameka, is there any other place you can think of? Have we checked all his spots? John keeps blowing up my phone. I've been hiding out at hotels, nervous to go home. I can't keep living like this. We have to face him sooner or later. I'm positive the only reason we're not dead is because of the respect he has for Andre."

"Keisha, he called me too," Sherrie said. "He asked me if I heard from you or Tameka. I lied and told him no, but I know he didn't believe me."

"Let's go to John's," Tameka said, throwing up her hands. "Fuck it, I got nothing to hide. It's like you said, Keisha, we can't keep living life in fear."

Keisha rolled her eyes and turned her head. *This bitch got balls today,* she thought, staring at pedestrians walking by. *If it weren't for her we wouldn't be in this situation.*

"Are you sure you want to do that, Tameka?" Sherrie asked.

"Yeah, I'm sure. Like I said, I have nothing to hide."

"Ok, then let's go." Keisha said. She was tired of playing hide and seek anyway.

Sherrie put the car in drive and they headed for John's office.

When they pulled up in front of John's warehouse, she turned off the car and exhaled loudly. She was nervous and it showed. She had been through a near-death experience when she was stabbed and she didn't want to face another one. But her loyalty was to her friends, so she was in just as deep as they were.

"Are y'all sure about going in there?" Keisha asked.

"Yes, I am," Tameka said.

"What about you, Sherrie?" Keisha reached out and held Sherrie's shaking hand.

Sherrie nodded.

Keisha looked at both of them. "Okay, let's go and bring your heat. When we go in here, there's a great possibility that we might not walk back out. So if we have to die, we're going out blazin' like real bitches do, taking at least one of them muthafuckas with us."

"I've never been so scared in my life," Sherrie confessed.

"Me either," Keisha said.

Tameka was quiet. She put her oversized sunglasses on, stepped out of car, and headed toward the warehouse.

Keisha and Sherrie got out and followed her.

To passersby, the trio looked like models on a mission.

The walk across the street seemed to take forever. Keisha's hands were trembling and sweaty and nervousness was still all over Sherrie's face. Tameka's expression was hidden by her glasses, but a vein popped in her temple.

They approach the big steel double doors to the warehouse and rang the bell.

"I guess this is how guys feel when they wake up and see John's guys," Keisha said. "They know it's their last moment on earth."

"I'd rather go unexpectedly than to know," Sherrie said. "This right here is killing me."

A raspy voice came through the intercom. "State your business."

"It's Keisha."

When the door buzzed, Tameka pushed it open, then turned to look at Sherrie and Keisha.

"Well, it's now or never," she said. "Here we go."

Keisha and Sherrie exchanged looks, then nodded.

A guard escorted them through the cold warehouse to John's desk and waved for them to take a seat. They sat in the chairs next to the desk and waited.

A few minutes later, John walked in, followed by his two six-foot-three, two hundred-pound guards. He was dressed in his usual slacks, button-down shirt with a loose tie, and dress shoes, but today, he also had on a shoulder holster and gun.

"Well, look who decided to come pay us a visit," he said with a smile.

He walked over to the girls and greeted each one of them with a kiss on the hand as he often did.

"Hello, ladies. I've been trying to contact you girls for days now. I call your phones, but no answer. No, let me correct that. I did speak to Sherrie. She was the only one who answered my call ... once." He looked at Keisha. "Where have you all been?" he asked calmly. "Is this the respect you give the person who's helping you get rich?" He walked over to Tameka's chair and sat on the armrest.

"John, we've been taking care of some business," Tameka explained.

"Oh, business, huh? Forgive me for assuming, but I thought I was you ladies' business."

"You are, but we had other things to handle," she said.

John stared at Keisha with a wry smile. She looked down at her nails, avoiding eye contact with him. The intensity of his stare made her nervous and her stomach turned. She had never wanted to get on his bad side. He's been good to her and treated with respect.

He looked back down at Tameka. "I have one question for you, Tameka. Was that June lying in that bed?"

"Yes," she answered.

She screamed when John grabbed her by the back of her neck, lifted her out of the chair, and slammed her head onto his desk, her glasses flying to the floor.

Holding her down with one hand, he used the other to take his .357 out of its holster and put the pistol to the side of her head.

Sherrie and Keisha jumped up, eyeing each other, and then looking back at John and Tameka. They had never seen this side of John and were scared for Tameka.

John turned to look at them. "Sit the fuck down. Don't make a move until I tell you to."

They sat back down immediately.

"And you shut the fuck up with all that screaming." Tameka stopped screaming, but kept weeping.

He placed his pistol to her left temple and bent down near her ear. In low voice, he said, "Don't fucking lie to me. Bitch, do you think I'm a fool? He lifted his head up and looked at Sherrie, and Keisha the pistol still pressed against Tameka's head. I told you bitches that I am God on these streets. I know *every* fucking thing that goes on. You think I don't know that you use to fuck with that nigga? Huh? Now tell me the fucking truth. You knew that wasn't him, didn't you?" Biting his lip, he pressed the barrel of the gun down harder.

"No, it was him in the bed when I left." Tameka sobbed, her face and upper body smashed against the desk.

"If that was him, how in the fuck is he alive? Are you telling me that my guys didn't do their jobs?"

Tameka cried harder. "I don't know, John. Please believe me. I left him in the bed." She looked at Keisha, her eyes begging for help.

"Tell me one reason why I shouldn't kill your ass right now."

"Because I did what I was suppose to do, John."

Keisha couldn't take it anymore. She stood up. One of the guards walked over by her, motioning for her to sit back down. She put her hands up, letting him know that she don't have any wrong intentions.

"John, please don't," she pleaded. "Please don't shoot her. We'll get him. Please, trust me, baby, we'll take care of it."

John looked at her with disgust. "Is your fucking name Tameka?" He pulled back on his revolver.

Tameka closed her eyes and started praying.

Keisha looked at him, then at Tameka crying and praying for her life. Everything was going too fast. Her heart was thumping and she couldn't think.

She looked at Sherrie, then sized up the guards. She didn't know what to do; she just knew that she didn't want her friend's brains blown out. Seeing no other option, she pulled her pistol out and aimed it at John's head. Sherrie pulled hers and pointed it at the guards.

John was taken aback. He didn't think they had it in them to pull out on him. He smirked, somewhat pleased with what he'd created in them, but disappointed that they'd turned on him.

Abruptly, the smile vanished and his face contorted in fury. "So it's like that, Keisha?" he asked.

"I guess so. I can't let you kill my sister." Her hands shook so much she had to use both hands to hold the gun.

Furious, he raised his voice. "You're going to risk your life for this dumb bitch?" he shouted. "She's not your fucking sister. She put all our lives in danger for a punk-ass nigga who obviously don't give a fuck about her. And you still consider her your sister and are willing to die for her?"

"John, I'm sorry, and I beg you to *please* give us another week and we'll bring his body to you personally and pay you back your money with interest."

"Fuck a week. You have four days or I'm going to kill her ass and you two bitches."

He grabbed Tameka by her hair and yanked her off his desk, throwing her to the floor. Keisha helped her up and Sherrie followed them as they backed slowly out the door with their pistols still in position to fire.

Outside, they ran to the car.

"Hurry, Sherrie, get us the fuck out of here," Keisha screamed, hitting the dashboard and looking back to make sure John's guys weren't behind them.

Sherrie sped off, running a stop sign. Tameka sat in the back, crying.

"What the fuck? What did I get myself into?" Keisha rocked back and forth.

"I can't believe this shit," Sherrie said, on the verge of tears herself. "Tameka you better think hard about where June could be. Our lives are on the line."

"I have Sherrie," Tameka cried. "Thank you guys for saving my life. I thought I was about to die."

"John is still going to kill your ass and us for pulling out on him," Keisha barked. "We're marked women! What in the fuck don't you understand? This shit is not a game, it's our lives."

"I know," Tameka said, sobbing. "Don't y'all think I feel bad that we're in this situation? I'm doing everything that I can think of to get us out of it. Here it is, my two best friends thinking that I would put their lives on the line for a nigga. I love y'all like my flesh and blood. Y'all are the only muthafuckas I got in this world I can depend on."

She leaned back in her seat, her head turned toward the window, and wiped at the stream of tears running down her face. "Drop me off at the house so I can check on my son."

Sherrie pulled up in front of Tameka's house and parked behind Keisha's car.

Tameka got out and walked to Keisha's window. "I love y'all and I would never do anything to put any of us in danger. It hurts that y'all don't believe that."

Keisha sat silently, looking straight ahead.

"We believe you, Tameka," Sherrie said. "Go get some rest; you've been through a lot today. Call us later."

When Keisha continued to ignore her, Tameka sighed, then turned and walked toward the house.

Keisha watched her walk away. At this point, she didn't believe anything Tameka said. Everything in her told her that she was lying. Keisha knew firsthand the power of love and what it could make you to do, but she'd never thought her friend would be the cause of their deaths. Her best friend of almost twenty years might not be who they thought she was and she was risking their lives for a dude. The pain of knowing that was almost physical.

Sherrie interrupted Keisha thought. "Look at them all on your car. These damn kids don't respect nobody's property."

"I know. But I'm not going to say anything to them

because if one of them gets smart with me, I'm going to take my anger from Tameka out on them and it wouldn't be fair for me to break one of those lil' bitches backs."

Sherrie laughed as Keisha pressed the alarm button on her car and the girls scattered.

Keisha was silent for a moment before she spoke again. "Sherrie, you know her ass is guilty. She knew that wasn't him in that bed. I don't know who it was, but it damn sure wasn't June and she knows it. She never breaks down like she did the day he showed up."

"You're right." Sherrie sighed. "I don't think she's innocent either. But I don't think she thought that she was putting us in danger and that's what's bothering her."

"We need the truth. I'm going to pay Dawgface to follow her around. He does private investigating and we can trust him. I paid him to follow Dino for me and he never found out."

"Yeah, do that, Keisha, and let me know what you find out."

"I will. You be careful."

"You too."

Chapter 20

*T*wo days later, Keisha received a call from Dawgface. He had some information she wanted. She arranged to meet him at Daley's restaurant on 63rd and Cottage Grove. Unable to reach Sherrie, she went by herself.

At the restaurant, she scanned the room, looking for Dawgface. He spotted her and waved.

He's such a handsome guy, she thought, walking toward him. She had always liked the way he dressed and carried himself. Fair-skinned guys weren't her normal cup of tea, but Dogface had a swag that couldn't be ignored. Tall and muscular with dreamy eyes, he had his pick of women. She just couldn't understand why such a handsome man would call himself "Dawgface."

He greeted her with his usual pleasant smile and a hug. "Would you like something to eat?" he asked, sitting back down. "Or something to drink?"

Keisha sat down across from him. "No, thank you. I don't have much of an appetite."

Getting straight to business, he reached into his satchel, pulled out a big yellow envelope, and slid it across the table to her.

"All the information you wanted to know is inside here. I'll keep digging for more."

"Thank you," she said, looking down at the envelope. The truth was right there in front of her. An overwhelming feeling of nervousness consumed her.

After she'd paid Dawgface and he left, she looked down at the envelope again, reluctant to open it. Deciding she didn't want to do it alone, she tried calling Sherrie again. There was still no answer.

Taking a deep breath, she picked the envelope up and ripped it open. Pulling out the contents, her heart dropped into her stomach.

There it was in black and white — Tameka kissing June by a building.

She looked at the date and time stamped in the corner of the photo. *That dirty bitch!* It was the date they'd gone to face John. She flipped through each picture, tears forming in her eyes. It was one thing for her to think Tameka was guilty, but getting proof of it brought on a whole other level of pain. There was even a picture of Tameka, June, and Emonie together.

Her phone rang and she looked at the caller ID. It was Tameka. Unable to deal with her, Keisha sent the call to voicemail. It immediately rang again and she ignored it again. She needed to pull herself together before she could deal with her *friend*.

Tameka kept calling.

Finally, Keisha answered. "What's up, Tameka?"

Tameka was screaming and talking fast.

"Slow down. I can't understand what you are saying," Keisha said.

"Big Man is dead!"

"What? How? Never mind. I'm on my way."

Keisha tried calling Sherrie again, still no answer.

Running to her car, she tried calling Sherrie again, but there was still answer. She was starting to get worried. It wasn't like Sherrie not to answer her phone. *I wonder where she is.*

When Keisha got to Tameka's, the house was full of people. Emonie was walking around with his bottle, unaware that he would never see the man he knew as Daddy again.

The rumor was that Big Man had been at a stop light on 63rd and Greenwood when some dudes off Kimbark rode up on him and shot the car up.

Tameka was out of it and couldn't seem to pull herself together.

"Let's take a ride to get some fresh air," Keisha suggested. She wanted to get her calmed down and then confront her with Sherrie.

Arriving at Sherrie's apartment, they saw her car parked out front. They knocked on the door and called her phone, but still didn't get an answer. Worried, they found the maintenance man and asked him to open the door. He refused until Keisha gave him a hundred dollars.

Walking into Sherrie's apartment was like stepping into the aftermath of a bar fight. Tables and chairs had been turned over, lamps broken, and pictures torn from the walls. They went through the rooms, looking for Sherrie. They finally found her battered, bruised, and unresponsive on the bathroom floor.

"Call nine-one-one right now," Keisha yelled to the maintenance man, dropping to the floor next to Sherrie.

"Right now!"

Tameka paced the floor, mumbling and shaking her head in disbelief.

The man ran into the living room to look for the phone. He came back with the smashed cordless phone in his hand.

Keisha got to her feet. "Tameka, help me get her into the car."

With the maintenance man's help, they managed to get Sherrie's unconscious body in the car safely. Driving high speed on local streets, running red lights, and dodging pedestrians, they screeched into the hospital parking lot with a police car chasing behind them. Keisha jumped out in ran through the emergency room entrance.

"Help me, please, somebody," she begged.

She ran over to the nurse's station. "Help me! My friend is in my car and she's unconscious." The nurse called for assistant they got her out of the car and rushed her to back to a room.

The police woman who'd been chasing them questioned Tameka and Keisha about Sherrie and handed Keisha a speeding ticket. Keisha looked at her in disbelief before balling the ticket up and walking away.

Keisha went back and forth to the information desk asking the same question. They wanted to know how Sherrie was doing.

After hearing the clerk say yet again that she had no update, Keisha got pissed off and snapped at her. "What's the purpose of having an information desk if you never know shit?" Finally, a nurse walked from the back. She told them that Sherrie had been sexually assaulted and beaten into a coma.

Keisha's knees got weak and she collapsed. The nurse and Tameka assisted her to a chair. Once she regained her strength, she was ready to see Sherrie.

"Can I please go see her?" she asked the nurse.

Seeing how upset and worried they were, the nurse reluctantly agreed. "Yes, you can, but only for a few minutes."

Tameka decided to leave, saying it was too much for her.

Days went by with Sherrie remaining in her coma. Keisha and Mary, Sherrie's mom, sat at her bedside day and night, waiting for her to open her eyes.

Tameka and her mom, Jennifer, visited daily. Tameka was still dealing with the death of Big Man and planning his funeral.

Keisha sat holding Sherrie's hands, wanting desperately for her friend to open her eyes. "I don't know who did this to you," she whispered, "but when I find out, I'm gonna kill 'em. Now, wake up and tell me who did this. Bad bitches don't die young; they die old with no regrets. We just started living, so you have to make it."

Mary and Jennifer walked in. Sherrie's mother hugged her Bible close to her chest and Tameka's mother held her up.

Keisha couldn't bear to see the pain in Mary eyes any longer, so she left. After four days straight, she needed to go home and shower.

After they'd talked to John, she'd checked out of the hotel and moved back home. Pulling up in front of her condo, she frowned, seeing that her balcony door was open. Apprehensive, she drove around the building and sneaked in the back door with her pistol ready to unload. She searched the house and found it empty. Nothing was out of place but her visitor had left her a note.

I enjoyed the virgin. You're next!

Tearing it up, she grabbed some of her things and left. She had no one to turn to. Andre was still locked up and she didn't want to involve Sincere. With no other options, she checked into another hotel.

Chapter 21

After showering and getting some sleep, Keisha phoned John.

"Hello, John. I'm sure you heard about Sherrie."

"Hello, Keisha, and, yes, I did."

Keisha got straight to the point. "Did you have anything to do with it?"

"I told you that I would give y'all four days and that's what I meant. I'm a man of my word. We both know who did it and I know where he is."

Keisha's other line rang and she looked at the caller ID. It was Dawgface.

"Excuse me, John, but I have take this call."

"No problem, I'll hold."

Keisha clicked to the other line. "What's up, Dawgface? Did you find out anything new?"

"Yeah, an address." He gave her an address and disconnected the call.

Going back to John, Keisha explained everything that had happened and gave him the address she'd just received. It was the same address he had. He told her he'd have two of his boys meet her at her hotel at sundown to go with her.

They were parked outside of the address when Keisha spotted Tameka pulling up. She felt as if she'd been punched in the stomach as they watched her best friend enter the house, using a key as if she lived there.

After waiting an hour, she convinced the guys to let her go in by herself first. After screwing a silencer on her gun, she crawled in through an open window and crept carefully into the apartment. She heard sounds behind the bedroom's closed door. Kicking it open, she ran in with her gun ready.

June jumped up, naked, and reached for his gun.

Keisha shot him in the hand. The gun failed on the floor. "I don't think you want to do a foolish thing like that."

A naked Tameka clutched a sheet, covering herself. "I'm sorry, Keisha. I know what you're thinking. He didn't do that to Sherrie."

Keisha turned to her, keeping her gun aimed at June. When she spoke, her voice was tinged with anger and sarcasm. "Isn't that funny how one brain can think for two people? You played us for this trifling-ass nigga?"

"I just couldn't do it, Keisha, I love him. He's Emonie's father."

"Bitch, I don't want to hear that shit. What about us? Our bond. Sisters, right? Friends to the end. A big ass lie, huh, Tameka?" Keisha said pointing her gun at them both.

Tameka started crying. "I do love you and Sherrie…"

"Shut the fuck up! We put our lives on the line for you. Sherrie is in a fucking coma because of you. You don't give a fuck. You put our lives on the line for a piece of dick."

"I can pay you," June offered, holding his bleeding hand.

"Pay this, bitch." Keisha said with venom in her voice.

"No, Keisha, no," Tameka wailed just as Keisha pulled the trigger and unloaded on him.

His lifeless body fell over to the side of the bed on the floor. A naked Tameka ran over to his side. Lifting his head onto her lap she cried. She picked up his gun and pointed at Keisha.

"Oh, you're going to shoot me, Tameka? You're going to pull out on me? After all we've been through?"

"I love you, Keisha, I do," Tameka sobbed. "But I love him with every ounce of my being."

Still pointing her gun at Keisha with one hand, she used her other to wrap the sheet around herself before scooting to the side of the bed where June's body lay and sliding down beside him. Looking at him with a sad smile, she stroked the side of his face. "Have you ever felt like you can't go on without someone? Like you can't laugh? Hell, you can't breathe. Every thought is about that person. That's how I feel. You never felt that way, have you, Keisha?"

Overcome with grief, she fell silent. "You don't feel," she said bitterly, looking back at Keisha. "You don't care. You don't have an emotional bone in your body. All you care about is money, Keisha. You stayed in an abusive relationship with Dino fucking your mom right under your nose for money. *You* are the reason that we're in the mess. You and your love for money and power."

"If I didn't care for you, I wouldn't be here," Keisha

yelled. "I would've let John kill your stupid ass. No, I don't care about a man. Fuck a nigga. They don't give a fuck about me, so why should I give a fuck about them? "

"Keisha, I never had a man love me like June, not even my father."

Keisha shook her head. "That's not love, Tameka. He used you. He didn't love you."

"Don't say that. He did love me," Tameka insisted. "We were going to Las Vegas to get married—me, him, and Emonie. See, here's my ring." Tameka held out her left hand for Keisha to see it. "You messed everything up. First Big Man, now you."

"So, you killed the man who truly loved you for this sorry piece of shit who didn't give a fuck about you?"

"Stop talking about my fiancé like that!" Tameka's gun wavered. "I had to kill Big Man, he wouldn't let me go."

"You know what?" Keisha said coldly. "Fuck you. Do what you gonna do. I'm tired of this shit. If you're going to shoot me, shoot me."

Fresh tears ran down Tameka's face. "You're my sister, I could never shoot you. I love you. But how can I go on living without my heart?"

She brought the gun to her head and closed her eyes. "Take care of our son." She squeezed the trigger.

Keisha lunged toward her. "No, Tameka, no!" She dropped to the floor and pulled Tameka into her arms, rocking back and forth and crying. Get up, Tameka. Please get up. I forgive you. I didn't mean what I said. Please Tameka don't die." Tameka took her last breath.

John's guys came rushing in and found her crying and holding Tameka.

"Come on, Keisha," one of the guys said. "We have to get out of here before the cops come."

Pulling the sheet more tightly around Tameka and smoothing it, Keisha shook her head. "No. I can't leave her. You go."

"Keisha, she's gone. You have to leave."

"I don't want to," she sobbed.

He looked at her for a few seconds, feeling sorry for her, then gently pulled her away from the body, picked her up and carried her out against her will.

Keisha gave John seventy thousands dollars to cover what they owed him plus interest. He gave her twenty back.

"Keisha, you're a strong young lady who's been through a lot more then you should have. But listen to me closely, you have to learn to trust, love and let go so you can be happy. Everybody isn't out to destroy you. Take care of yourself."

He kissed her softly on the lips and left.

She went to the hospital to see Sherrie.

"Sherrie, everything is safe now. You can wake up."

A loud beeping sound went off and nurses came running into the room.

"Move back," one of them instructed.

"What's going on?" Keisha asked

"You have to step out the room."

"Keisha was pushed out of the room as different machines were wheeled in and strapped to Sherrie.

Fifteen minutes later, the door opened and the doctors and nurses filed from the room. Keisha caught of a glimpse of Sherrie on the bed, the sheet pulled up to cover her face.

She felt like the wind had been knocked out of her. "I can't breathe." She gasped for breath. "Help me, I can't breathe."

A nurse sat her down in a chair and told her to take long, deep breaths. When Keisha was breathing normally again, the nurse asked Keisha if she had someone to come get her.

Keisha looked at her with tears in her eyes and shook her head no. For the first time in her life, she was truly alone.

Chapter 22

*J*ennifer and Mary decided to have Tameka and
Sherrie's funeral together. Everybody from their
neighborhood and some from other hoods were there
to show their respect. Many wore shirts, hats, or jackets
with Sherrie and Tameka's pictures on them that read,
"*R.I.P. Ghetto Beauties.*"

Keisha spared no expense. She made sure her friends
would have the most talked about homegoing ever, a
grand exit befitting the queens they were.

Sherrie and Tameka looked at peace in their matching pearl white caskets with gold trim. They were sur-
rounded by beautiful flower arrangements that John had
sent. Pictures of them at different ages hung throughout
the funeral home and a red carpet lay from their caskets
to the door.

Sherrie's hair was styled in its usual short, tapered
cut with a few curls at the top. She wore a white silk
V-neck dress and necklace with a cross around her neck.
Tameka had been dressed in a cream satin and chiffon
strapless dress with a shawl. Her long black tresses were
loosely curled, perfectly framing her heart-shaped face.
Her hands had been placed across her chest, holding a

picture of Emonie and displaying her cushion-cut engagement ring.

Every seat was filled; people were standing against the walls. When it was time to view the bodies, the line of people extended from the casket to outside the building and around the corner.

Sincere's niece, Tatierra, sang "Precious Lord" and brought everyone to tears. Keisha stared at the coffins with tears pouring down her face, cradling Emonie in her lap.

When the service ended, Sincere took Emonie outside and Keisha sat in the chapel alone. A large part of her had died with her friends. Realizing she would never see them again, grief engulfed her anew and she slumped over, her head in her lap.

A hand touched her hair, then moved to rub her back. A soft voice spoke, while caressing her back.

"Cry not for me, I'm gone to be with my father. Grieve if you will, but not for long. For with our love I was blessed for many years. I am at peace; my soul is finally at rest." Keisha recognized the voice and the prayer. *It can't be.* She sat up and joined in.

"Please don't stress over me, wipe your tears. I feel no pain. I'm in heaven where's there's eternal happiness and no fear. Celebrate my life. I now suffer not."

That was the prayer Isabella had taught her when her Chico died.

"Mom," Keisha said, her voice barely a whisper.

Isabella wiped her daughter's tears and kissed her on the cheek. "Don't you worry, baby, they're gone to a better place."

Keisha hadn't seen her mother in almost three years.

Isabella looked healthy and drug-free. She looked like the mom she had once adored and respected.

She got up and threw her arms around her mother and squeezed her tight.

Isabella hugged her back. "Baby, look at you. You're just as gorgeous as I remembered. I know how much you loved Tameka and Sherrie and I'm so sorry they're gone. And I'm sorry for all the pain and embarrassment I caused you over the years. Please forgive me."

Keisha wiped her eyes and sniffed. "I know you are Mom. I forgive you."

When she'd composed herself, Keisha went outside and released eighteen doves into the air, one for each year that the three had been friends.

After the funeral, she didn't feel like being bothered with anyone. Needing time to herself, she decided to skip the repast.

She stood for a moment, watching Isabella, Jennifer, and Mary. For the first time in a decade, all their parents were together and supporting one another. Regardless of the circumstances, she was pleased. She knew Tameka and Sherrie would have loved to that the three former friends had reunited.

She interrupted them to tell them she was leaving. Isabella hugged her and gave her a piece of paper with her contact information.

"Call me, I'm here for you. Your mother is back." She looked into Keisha's teary brown eyes and repeated it. "Your mother is back."

Isabella pulled her daughter into her arms and held her tightly. Tears fell from her eyes. She didn't want to let her daughter go.

Keisha pulled away, telling her that she loved her and would call her later. She hurried to her car, ignoring the people who called her name. Inside the car, she lay her head on the steering wheel and let out a big sigh.

A man knocked on her window and asked if she was okay, she looked up at him and nodded before starting the car and pulling off.

With no destination in mind, she got on the freeway and headed east. She didn't know where she was going; she just wanted to get as far away from the Southside of Chicago as possible.

She drove until her gas gauge beeped. Finding a gas station next door to a bar, she pulled in. After she filled up her tank, she went inside the bar and took a seat. She was tired and needed to rest her eyes for a bit.

The bar was small and outdated and it stank. It smelled like beer, peanuts, and ass.

Keisha turned up her nose. "Excuse me, where am I?" she asked the bartender.

"You're in the Motor City, The bartender said proudly."

Wow, she thought. She looked down at her watch. *I've been driving for over four hours.* She hadn't realized how many hours had gone by or the distance she'd driven.

A group of three guys and two girls sitting at a table across from her caught her attention. The girls was kissing and grinding on each other while the guys cheered them on.

Those cheap tramps, she thought.

The dark-skinned guy with a low-cut Ceasar and a huge rock in his left ear saw her watching them. He locked eyes with Keisha, smiled and raised his glass in her direction.

Not in the mood to talk or flirt, she quickly turned her head, ignoring him.

After a few minutes, he walked over and said, "Excuse me, but do I know you?"

"No, I don't think so." She got up and headed to the door.

He followed in pursuit. "This is a small world." He said with a cocky laugh.

"Excuse me?" she said. Uneasy, she turned to face him.

He got closer. "Long time no see."

"I'm sorry, but you must have me confused with someone else."

"No, I don't think so. I could never forget your face."

"I'm a model. You've probably seen me in a magazine or on a billboard. I'm sure we never met."

"No, that's not it," he insisted, staring at her. Recognition lit his eyes.

Keisha dug around in her purse, searching for her gun. *Why in the hell did I buy this big ass saddlebag?* she asked herself. She was jittery. She hoped he thought she was reaching for her keys.

"Up until this very moment, I wasn't exactly sure, but now I'm positive of who you are." He pulled out his piece and pointed it at her. "You're the bitch from the Chi that set my cousin up. Pull your hand out that muthafucking bag. Yo ass not slick."

Keisha pulled her hand out of her purse. She looked around to see if there was anybody around. There was little light and the street was empty and quiet, as if they were alone on another planet. Though she'd been threatened before, this was the first time in her life that she'd had a gun aimed at her and she was terrified. She stared at it, her eyes wide, trying to figure out her next move.

She stuck to her story of mistaken identity. "You've got me confused with someone else."

He shook his head. "I'd never forget your face."

Seeing no other choice, she dropped her purse and ran. Almost simultaneously, she heard a shot and felt a burning pain in her arm.

"Stop right now," he ordered. "The next shot is your head.

She stopped and turned, holding her arm.

He walked closer to her, looking her up and down licking his lips. "You are one bad bitch. I never cared too much for my cousin. He always thought he was better than my brother and me. He treated us like shit most of the time. But I love my Auntie and to see the pain in her eyes you caused..."

"I didn't kill your cousin. And if you didn't care for him, why harm me for something you think I did to someone you didn't like? Come on, baby, why don't you just let me go?" Keisha's heart pounded and her legs were like jelly. She struggled to keep from trembling.

"You must be crazy, bitch."

"Baby, I'm not crazy. I just think I can be more valuable to you alive than dead."

"How's that?"

"I see you're a man of power. I peeped all your flunkies in there catering to you, and those girls trying to seduce you with girl-on-girl foreplay. But your eyes were on me from the time I sat at the bar," She lowered her voice seductively. "You want me. And I love a man with your power and ambition, one who pays attention to me and knows how to get what he wants."

He nodded and curled one side of his lips "All that sounds good, ma. I do love a woman like yourself—a sassy, classy, smart, stunning gangsta bitch. Hell, I haven't been able to get you out of my mind since the first day I saw you. I don't know if it was because you killed my cousin or because I wanted to fuck you myself that night."

Keisha smiled, her nervousness evaporating. "See, that's what I am saying, baby. Let's make this work out for both of us. I get you and you'll get me."

She let go of her arm and stepped closer to him. When he stepped back, she smiled. *This nigga has a gun and he shot me, but he's scared,* Keisha thought. *I'm a bad bitch.*

"I know you're not scared of little old me? You're the one with the pistol."

This time, when she moved closer, he stayed where he was. Pulling his lips to hers, she kissed him. When she felt him kiss her back, she directed his hand underneath her dress. He moved her panties to the side and stuck a finger into her wetness, mimicking his tongue move- ments in her mouth. She stepped back, pulled his hand up and licked the finger that had been in her and then put it to his mouth.

Licking his finger, he pushed her back against the building and slowly brought his pistol up to her chest.

"You do taste good and I want you with every bone in my body, but I could never trust a bitch like you. When the power and money is gone, you will be too."

She tried to knock the gun away, then turned and ran.

He fired.

Keisha fell to the ground, her back burning. Gasping and unable to catch her breath from the pain, she tried to crawl away, still trying to escape.

A hand grabbed her roughly and flipped her over.

He bent down, kissed her forehead, "Rest in peace, my ghetto beauty."

Through tears, she saw him aim the gun at her head.

A shot rang out and everything went black. Somewhere in the darkness, she heard footsteps running away.

In the back of my mind, I always knew this day would come.

We had a ball, but all the shit I've done, the money, house, car, clothes, trips, and jewelry—none of it was worth this.

What a price to pay. I lost my two best friends because of my greed. They were happy, but I wanted more.

I don't want to die, God.

Father, I believe in you, help me. Save me. Cover me with your blood, Jesus.

If you let me make it through this alive, I promise I'll never...

Reading Group Guide
For
Beauty N' Betrayal **by Sincere**

The suggested questions are intended to enhance your group's reading of this book.

1. Who was your favorite character(s) and why? Who was your least favorite and why? Describe each character in one word.

2. Keisha's life changed when she discovered Isabella and Dino's affair. How was she affected? Was her retaliation warranted? Why or why not? How would you have responded?

3. What do you think of Andre killing the guy while Keisha was in the car? If you were her, would you have turned him in?

4. What do you think of Keisha and Andre's relationship? Do you think they had genuine love for one another as family? Why or why not? After Keisha got word of the hit out on her, she contacted him for help? Would you have done the same?

5. What was your take on Keisha, Tameka, and Sherrie's friendship? Do you think they allowed money, love, and power to come between them? Who do you think was the most loyal?

6. Do you think Keisha was insensitive of Tameka's feelings for June? Why or why not? Does this say anything about Keisha's character and how she values their friendship?

7. What are your thoughts on Sherman? What are your thoughts about John asking Keisha to be his woman instead of just his thrill? Which of the men do you think would have been a better match for her? Why?

8. While outwardly displaying loyalty to her friends, Tameka was hiding June and plotting to elope. Do you think she was selfish and intentionally put Keisha and Sherrie's lives in danger?

9. At the funeral, Isabella and Keisha are reunited. Would you have forgiven Isabella if you were Keisha? Do you think she caught Keisha at a vulnerable moment?

10. Keisha loves the finer things in life and refuses to downsize her lifestyle. What do you think of her actions to maintain her luxurious standard of living?

11. Did you expect the book to end the way it did? Why? How would you have liked to see it end?

ORDER FORM

TRJ PUBLISHING
P.O. BOX 3342
CULVER CITY, CA 90230-9998
WWW.BEAUTYNBETRAYAL.COM

PLEASE SEND: _____copies of *Beauty N' Betrayal* to:

NAME _____

EMAIL_____

ADDRESS_____

CITY_____ STATE_____ ZIP_____

BASIC ORDER:
A: NO. OF COPIES   _____ (AS PER ORDER)

B: COST PER COPY $_____ (USA $14.95; CAN $16.95) (Inmate $12.95)

C: TOTAL BASE COST $_____ (C= A x B)

SHIPPING:
D: $3.00 PER BOOK $_____ (D = A x $3.05; postage, packaging)

TOTAL OF ORDER: $_____ (Total= C + D)

PAYMENT:
    o   Check enclosed
    o   Credit Card
    o   Money Order enclosed

CREDIT CARD NUMBER: _____EXP. DATE: _____/_____

CARDHOLDER NAME: _____

CARDHOLDER SIGNATURE: _____
If billing address is different from shipping address write both on this form.

THANK YOU FOR YOUR ORDER